THE
RETURN JOURNEY

MAEVE BINCHY

—THE—
RETURN JOURNEY

Delacorte Press

Published by
Delacorte Press
Bantam Doubleday Dell Publishing Group, Inc.
1540 Broadway
New York, New York 10036

Library of Congress Cataloging in Publication Data
Binchy, Maeve.
    The return journey / Maeve Binchy.
        p.   cm.
    ISBN 0-385-31506-6
    1. Ireland—Social life and customs—Fiction.   I. Title.
PR6052.I7728R48   1998
823'.914—dc21   97-52624
                                                    CIP

Manufactured in the United States of America
Published simultaneously in Canada

April 1998

10   9   8   7   6   5   4   3   2   1
BVG

To dearest Gordon
With all my love

CONTENTS

THE
RETURN JOURNEY

Mother darling,
It's even more green and beautiful than you said. Having a really wonderful time. Will write soon. Keep well and happy.

Gina

Freda,

The card I sent yesterday was for the neighbors. Or rather for you and your paranoia about the neighbors. Anyway its purpose was that it could be left around and looked at, spied on, and inspected by them. The truth is that the place is a shambles, it's raining so hard I can't see whether it's green or yellow. The truth is that I still feel hurt and unhappy and not at all like writing letters. The truth is that I must care about you a great deal, otherwise why am I letting that call from the airport get to me so badly? I believed you when you said you'd watch for the mail. I will write, but just now there's nothing to say.

Try not to worry about what people think and say. Honestly, they aren't thinking and saying much about us at all. They have their own problems.

Gina

Darling Gina,

You called me Freda instead of Mom. I wondered about that for a long while. I suppose it means you're growing up, growing away. I told myself it meant you liked me more, thought of me as an equal, a friend. Then I told myself that it meant you liked me less, that you were distancing your-self.

For someone who claims there is nothing to say, you sure have a lot to say. You say I am paranoid about the neighbors. Well, let me tell you that Mrs. Franks came in to say

4

she couldn't help reading your nice postcard and wasn't it wonderful that Gina was having such a good time. So! Do they look or do they not?

You say that you are upset by the call from Kennedy Airport. It was you who called me, Gina. I just said write me often. You are the one who was crying, I was the one who says what any normal mother says to a daughter traveling abroad . . . going to Europe. I said, I'd like it if you wrote to me, is that so emotionally draining? Does it deserve the lecture, the sermon . . . the order not to live my life by other people's dictates?

But I only say all this so that you'll know I'm still me, still the same prickly jumpy thin-skinned mother I always was. I like you to call me Freda. Don't stop now because you think I've taken it and run with it, that I've read into it more than there is. And don't stop writing to me, Gina. You know I didn't want you to go to Ireland. But I did say . . . I always said it was an unreasonable feeling on my part. There are so many things I want to hear about Ireland, and so many I don't.

I think I want you to tell me that it's beautiful and sad and that I did the only possible thing by leaving it. And leaving it so finally. I think that's what I want you to say in your letters. And when you come home. I love you, Gina, if that's not too draining.

Freda

I'm calling you nothing in this letter in case we get another long analysis. I had an odd day today. I left the B and B, which is fine, small room, small house, nice woman, kept telling me about her son in Boston who's an Illegal. I thought she meant the IRA, but she meant working in a bar without a proper visa or a green card. Anyway I was walking down the street, small houses, hundreds of kids *roaming round when school's out, the country is like a big school playground in many ways. And I saw a bus. It said "Dunglass." It was half full. I put out my hand. And it stopped. I asked the driver "Where is Dunglass?" And he told me. . . . But I said isn't Dunglass not a house, a big house. He said no, it was a town. Mom, why didn't you tell me it was a town? What else did you not tell me? I got off the bus. I told him I had changed my mind.*

Back at the B and B the woman was happy. She had heard from her son the Illegal. It was cold in Boston, lots of ice and snow. I asked her about Dunglass. She said it was a village. She said it was a nice kind of a place, quiet, peaceful but not a place to go in the middle of winter. It would scald your heart, she said. Why didn't you say it was a village that would scald your heart? Why did you let me think for years that it was a big old house with Dunglass on the gate. You even told me what it meant. Dun a fort and Glass meaning Green. That much is true, I checked. But what else is?

Gina

Gina my love,
I wish you'd call. I tried to get a number for you, but they don't do street listings like we do. It's five days since you wrote. It will be five days until you get this, ten days could have changed everything. You may have been there by now, for all I know.

I never told you it was a house. Never. Our house didn't have a name that's all, it was a big house, it did have gates, it was the biggest house in Dunglass, which wasn't saying anything great. I just didn't talk about any of it. There are things in your life we don't go over and over. Go see Dunglass, go on a day when there is light and even watery winter sunshine. Go on a day when you might be able to walk down by the lake. Go see the house. Your grandmother is dead and in the churchyard on the hill. There is no one who will know you. But tell people if you want to. Tell them your mother came from Dunglass and left it. I don't think you will tell them. You are always saying that most people are not remotely interested in the lives and doings of others.

I love you and I will tell you anything you want to know.

Your mother Freda, in case you have forgotten my name.

Freda,
Stop playing silly games. And let us stop having an argument by mail. Yes, I will go to Dunglass. When I'm ready.

And don't talk to me about my grandmother. She was never allowed to be a grandmother to me. Her name was not spoken to me, I got no letters, no presents . . . there were no pictures of me in a Grannie's Brag Book on this side of the Atlantic. The woman who lies in the churchyard on the hill is your mother. That's the relationship. You might as well face it. Her name was Mrs. Hayes. That's all I know. You were Freda Hayes, so my grannie was Mrs. Hayes. Don't lecture me, Freda, about forgetting your name, you never even told me hers.

Gina

Dear Gina,

I have begun this letter twelve times, this is the thirteenth attempt, I will send it no matter what. Her name was Annabel. She was tall and straight. She walked as if she owned Dunglass. And in a way she did. It was her family who had the big house. My father married in, as they say. I never knew why they sent me away to boarding school, why they made me leave such a lovely home. Peggy who looked after me used to whisper about rows, and ornaments being broken, but I couldn't believe that my dad could be like Peggy said he was, two men, one man sober and another man drunk. Everyone admired my mother, because she ran the place. Even after my father went away she never asked for sympathy. She was cold, Gina, she made herself cold and hard. She used to say to me that we didn't need their sympathy, their pity. We needed only their admiration. Perhaps some of that has rubbed off on me, perhaps I care too much about people thinking well of me, rather than being natural. She had only one daughter, as I have. We could have been more alike than I ever realized. I can't write any more. I love you. I wish you were here. Or I were there. No, I don't wish I were there, I can never go to Dunglass. But I want you to go and to get some peace and some of your history from it.

Freda

Dear Freda,

Thanks for your letter. I think I'll cool it a bit on all the emotion. Don't forget I have Italian blood as well. The mix is too heady. I could explode. The days are getting brighter, I've been to Wicklow a lot, it's so beautiful . . . and I went farther south, Wexford . . . the riverbank is like something from a movie . . . and Waterford. The Illegal is home from Boston, his name is Shay. He is very funny about Boston, but I think he wasn't happy there, he says his dream is to have a little cottage in Wicklow, and write songs. It's not a bad dream. I have no dreams really.

I'm doing an extramural course in the university about Irish history. It was full of dreams. I'll give you the telephone number in case you're lonely and sad. But don't call just for talking. It's very artificial.

Shay says that when he and his mother used to talk, they both put the phone down feeling like hell. We don't want

*that, Freda. Now that we're rubbing along OK. Yes, of
course I love you.*

Gina

Gina,
*It was so different then. You can't imagine. I remember the
year I met your father. All right. All right. The year I met
Gianni . . . the man I married. Does that satisfy you? It
seemed like as if there was nothing but big funerals that
year. Brendan Behan died, Sean O'Casey died. And Roger
Casement . . . no, I know he didn't die then, but his body
was brought back to Ireland, that's when I met Gianni. I
tried to explain it to him. We sat in a café, it was a cold wet
day. He was an Italian American. He tried to explain to
me about Vietnam. It was 1964. I told Gianni all about
the Irish troops leaving on the peacekeeping mission in Cyprus and I showed him where they were building the new
American Embassy. And the Beatles went to America that
year . . . it seems like a hundred years ago.*

*And Gianni wanted to know where I was from, so I took
him home to Dunglass. And Mother laughed at him because he told her how poor his parents had been when they
got the boat from Italy.*

*And I didn't want to sleep with him, Gina, I was
twenty-three like you are now, but in those days we were so
different. Not just me . . . everyone, I promise you. But I
hated Mother so much for scorning him. And I despised her*

10

for saying that she hadn't gone through so much just for me to throw myself away on the son of a chambermaid and a hall porter. Gianni had told with pride how his parents, your grandparents, had got these jobs. And Mother said it in front of Peggy. Just letting Peggy know how little she thought of Peggy's role in life.

I was glad, Gina, I was glad when I was pregnant, even though I was frightened at the thought of living with Gianni forever. I felt it wouldn't last, that we didn't know each other, and that when we did we might be sorry. But we were never sorry, we had you.

And you will admit that, difficult as I have been, and stubborn, I have never said anything bad about your father. He thought he could live in Dunglass and marry in like my father had. But my mother hunted him, and she hunted me too because I wouldn't stay one minute to listen to her harsh words.

I left my room as it was, my books and letters and papers. I don't know what happened to them. Ever. I closed that door and never opened it.

When Gianni left me I didn't feel as sad as people thought. I knew it would happen. I had my home in America, my daughter, my job in the bookshop, my friends. I may marry again.

I won't, of course, but I say to myself cheerfully like Peggy used to say it may be a sunny day after all, little Freda. My heart is heavy when I think of Peggy. I didn't write to her because I didn't write to the big house, it would have been twisting a knife too harshly into Mother.

Her name was Peggy O'Brien, Gina, they lived in a

cottage by the lake. I tried to write after Mother died. But there weren't any words. You were always good with words, Gina.

Love *Freda*

This is a postcard of Dunglass village. I bought it in a Dublin shop. Has it changed much, Mother? I'm going there tomorrow. I'll write and tell you everything. I miss you.

Gina

The time gap is too long. I called you. Shay's mother told me you were still away. You didn't say you were taking Shay with you. It's nearly a quarter of a century since I took Gianni there. Are we going to repeat history all over again? Dunglass hasn't changed very much. I had forgotten it was so small. I wait to hear anything you may write.

Dearest Freda,
Your letter was cold, there were no dears or darlings or loves anywhere. Are you afraid that like my mother and my grandmother, I will marry hastily the wrong man, who will leave me as happened to you and to Annabel? I went to

her grave and I laid a big bunch of spring flowers on it. The countryside is glorious. There were little ducklings on the lake, and moorhens and two big swans. You never told me any of that. You never told me that you had a pony and that you fell off and broke your arm. You never told me about Peggy's big soft bosom where I cried like you cried. She bought a lot of your things at the auction. She said she didn't want strangers picking up your books and your treasures. She called them treasures, Freda, and she has them in a room. Waiting for you to come home and collect them. She was left nothing in the will. It all went to charity. She bought them from her wages because she knew one day you'd come back.

I told her it would probably be in June. When the sun shines long hours over the lake and the roses are all out on her cottage. Not far from the one that Shay and I are looking at with our hearts full of hope.

Send me an open postcard to Shay's house so that his mother will know how much you and I love each other. See, I am like you after all. I want them to think well of us. In many ways I'm glad you kept it from me, it came as such a rainbow of happiness. But don't keep it from yourself anymore. There are no ghosts in Dunglass. Only hedges and flowers and your great friends Peggy, Shay, and

Gina

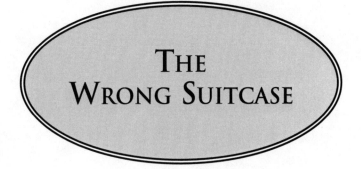

THE
WRONG SUITCASE

Annie checked in early. She had come out to the airport in plenty of time. None of this was going to be a hassle. Once she had taken her boarding card and seen the smart new case trundle off with its little tag telling it to go to London Heathrow, she sighed with relief; it was all happening now, nothing could stop it. She was going to have the luxury of really looking at the things in the duty-free shop for once, and maybe trying out a few of the perfumes on her wrist. She might even look at cameras and watches—not buy, but look.

Alan was late; he was always late checking in. But he had such a nice smile and looked so genuinely apologetic, nobody seemed to mind. They told him to go straight to the departure gate, and he did—well, more or less. They couldn't expect him to go through that duty-free without buying a bottle of vodka, could they? He had no sign of fuss or confusion; he slipped onto the plane last, but somebody had to come in last. He settled himself easily into his seat in executive class. With the ease of the frequent traveler, he had stowed his briefcase and vodka neatly above, fastened his safety belt in a way that the air hostess could see it was fastened, and he had opened his copy of *Time*. Another business trip begun.

Annie smiled with relief when she saw her case on the carousel at London Airport; she always half expected it to be left behind, like she expected the Special Branch men to call her in and ask her business in England and the Customs men to rip the case apart looking for concealed heroin. She was of a fearful nature, but she knew that and said it wasn't a bad way to be because it led to so many nice surprises when these things didn't happen. She took her case and went unscathed through Customs. She followed the signs for the Underground and got onto a train that she thought must be like a lift in the United Nations building: There were people of every nationality under the sun, and all of their suitcases had different little tags. She closed her eyes happily as the train rushed into London.

Alan reached out easily and took his case as it was about to pass by. He helped a family who couldn't cope with all their cases arriving at once. One by one he swung them off the conveyor belt, and when he took one that wasn't theirs he just swung it easily back again with no fuss. The woman gave him a very grateful smile. Alan had a way of looking better than other people's husbands. He bought an *Evening Standard* in the paper shop and settled himself into a taxi. He had already asked the taxi driver if he could have a receipt at the end of the journey; some of them could be grumpy, always better to say what you want at the start and say it pleasantly. Alan's motto. Alan's secret of success. It was sunset; he looked out briefly at the motorways and the houses with their neat gardens away in the distance. It was nice to be back in London where you didn't know everyone and everyone didn't know you.

The train took Annie to Gloucester Road, and she walked with a quick and happy step to the hotel, where she had stayed many times. The new suitcase was light to carry; it had been expensive, but what the hell—it would last forever. It was so nice, she had bought two of those little suitcase initials and stuck them on. "A.G." At first she wondered if this was a dead giveaway, wouldn't people know that they weren't married if they had different initials? But he had laughed at her and patted her nose, telling her that she was a funny little thing and had a fearful nature. And Annie Grant had agreed and remembered that most people didn't give a damn about that sort of thing nowadays. Most people.

The taxi took Alan to Knightsbridge and the hotel, where they remembered him or pretended to. He always said his name first, just in case. "Of course, Mr. Green," the porter said with a smile. "Good to have you with us again." Alan folded the receipt from the taxi driver into his wallet and followed the porter to the desk; his room reservation was in order. He made an elegant and flattering remark to the receptionist, which left her patting her hair with pleasure and wondering why the nice ones like Mr. Green didn't ask you out and the yucky ones slobbered all over you. Alan went up to his room and took a bottle of tonic from the minibar. He noticed it wasn't slimline, so he put it back and took soda. Alan was careful about everything.

Annie opened her case in the small hotel bedroom where she would spend one night. She would hang up her dresses to make sure the creases fell out. She would have a bath and use all those nice lotions and bath oils so that they didn't look brand new tomorrow. The key turned and she lifted the lid. There were no dresses and no shoes. Neither the two new nighties nor the very smart toilet bag with its unfamiliar Guerlain products were in the case. There were files and boxes and men's shirts and men's underpants and socks, and more files. Her heart gave several sharp sideways jumps, each one hurting her breast-bone. It had happened as she always knew it would happen one day. She had got the wrong case. She looked in terror and there were her initials; somebody else called AG had taken her case. "Oh my God," wept Annie Grant, "oh God, why did you let this happen to me? Why? I'm not *that* bad, God. I'm not hurting anyone else." Her tears fell into the suitcase.

Alan opened his case automatically. He would set his papers out on the large table and hang up his suits. Marie always packed perfectly; he had shown her how at an early stage. Poor Marie had once thought you just bundled things in any old how, but, he had explained reasonably, what was the point of her ironing all those shirts so beautifully if they weren't to come out looking as immaculate as they went in? He looked at the top layer of the case in disbelief. Dresses, underwear—female underwear neatly folded. Shoes in plastic bags, a flashy-looking sponge bag with some goo from a chemist in it. God almighty, he had taken the wrong case. But he couldn't have. It had his initials: A.G. He had been thinking that he must get better ones, these were a bit ordinary. God damn and blast it, why hadn't he got them at the time? For a wild moment he wondered if this was some kind of joke of Marie's; she had been very brooding recently and wanting to come on business trips with him.

21

uld she have packed a case for herself? But that was nonsense; these weren't Marie's things, these belonged to a stranger. Shit, Alan Green said aloud to himself over and over again. What timing. What perfectly bloody timing to lose his case on this of all trips.

It took Annie a tearful seventy minutes on the telephone and many efforts on the part of the airline and of the hotel to prevent her from going out to the airport before she realized that she would have to wait until the next morning. Soothing people in the hotel and in the airline said that it would certainly be returned the following day. She had only discovered an office address for Mr. Bloody Green, typed neatly and taped inside the lid of the case. An office long closed by now.

Tomorrow, the voices said, as if that was any help. Tomorrow he would have arrived expecting her to be in fine form and to have her things with her. They were going to go for a week's motoring holiday, the first time she was going to have him totally to herself. He was flying in from New York and would hire a car at Heathrow; he had told his boss the negotiations would take longer, he had told his wife . . . Who knew or cared what he had told his wife? But he would not be best pleased to spend the first day of their holiday in endless negotiations at the airport looking for her things. Was there no way she could find out where this idiot lived? If she phoned his home, even maybe his wife could tell her where he was staying. That was if his wife knew. If wives ever knew.

It took Alan five minutes to find the right person, the person who told them that there was no right person at this time of night, but to explain the machinery of the morrow. Yes, fine for those who hadn't arranged a breakfast meeting at seven-thirty A.M., before the shops were open, before he could get a clean shirt. And what was the point of a breakfast meeting without his papers? God rot this stupid woman with her cellophane bags and her tissue paper and her never-worn clothes. Her photograph album, for heaven's sake, and pages and pages of notes, a play of some sort. Hard-to-decipher writing, page after bloody page of it. But there was one page where it revealed the address of Miss Prissy A. Grant, whoever she was, and he was sure she *was* a Miss, not a Mrs. A letter addressed to her had "Ms." on it, but Alan had always noted that this was what single, not married, women called themselves. Unfortunately it had no address, or he could have sent for an Irish telephone directory and found her mother and father and got the hotel that their daughter was staying at. That's if she had told them. Nutty kind of girls who carry photograph albums, unworn clothes, and plays written in small cramped writing probably told their families nothing.

The man who ran the small hotel near Gloucester Road was upset for nice Miss Grant, who often came to spend a night before she went on her long trips to the Continent; she was a teacher, a very polite person always. He took her a pot of tea and some tomato sandwiches in her room. She cried and thanked him as if he had pulled her onto a life raft.

"Look through his things. You might discover where he is staying," he advised. Annie was doubtful. Still, as she ate the tomato sandwiches and drained the pot of tea she spread all the papers out on the small bed and read. She read of the plans that Mr. A. Green had been building up over the last two years. Plans which meant that by tomorrow he should be able to take over an agency for himself. If things went the way he hoped.

Mr. A. Green would return to Dublin at the head of his own company. The arguments were so persuasive that the overseas client would be very foolish not to accept A. Green's offer. There were photocopies of letters marked "For Your Eyes Only" . . . there were files with heavy underlining in thick felt pen, "Do not take to Office." A great deal of the correspondence was organized so that it showed A. Green's present employers, the people who were paying for this trip to London, in a very poor light. Annie sighed; she supposed that this was the world of business. At school you didn't go plotting against the geography mistress or getting the headmaster to lose confidence in the art teacher. But it seemed a bit sneaky.

Sometimes there were copies of letters his boss *was* shown pinned to those he had *not* been shown. It was masterly filing, and if you read the whole anthology, which up to now had presumably been for Alan Green's eyes only, it made a convincing case. Annie decided that A. Green was a bastard and he deserved to have lost his case and his deal. She hoped he would never find either. But then how would she get back what was hers? And God almighty, suppose he had read her diary.

Alan Green decided to hell with it, he couldn't bear the flat taste of the soda. He opened a calorie-packed tonic water from his minibar and decided that he would do this thing methodically. Look on it as a business problem. Right. He had left his name with the airline, if she called. Of course she would call. Stupid girl, why had she not called already? Stupid A. Grant. She was probably in a wine bar with an equally stupid teacher talking about plays and how to write them in longhand at great length and maximum stupidity. What kind of play was it, anyway? He began to read it. He read of her romance. . . . It wasn't a play, it was the real thing. This was a diary. It was more than a diary, it was a plan of campaign. It was dozens of different scenarios that could take place on this holiday.

There was the scene where he said he couldn't see her anymore, that his wife had given him an ultimatum. This creepy A. Grant had written out her lines for that one, several times over. Sometimes they were casual and see-if-I-care. Sometimes they were filled with passion, or threats: she would kill herself, let him wait. She had written the whole thing out as if it were a play, even with stage directions.

Alan decided that A. Grant was a raving lunatic and that whoever the poor guy she was going to meet was, he deserved to be warned about her.

He felt glad that she had lost this insane checklist of emotional dramas and how to play them; he was glad that all her finery had gone astray and that she would have to meet the guy as she was. He realized that she had probably done some kind of repair job and washed her tights and whatever just as he had washed the collar and cuffs of his shirt and the soles of his socks. Then he remembered with a lurch that she might have read his dossier on the company.

Annie suddenly remembered she hadn't told the man in the airport where she was staying. She had been too upset. Suppose Mr. Conniving Green had rung in with his whereabouts; they wouldn't have been able to contact her. She telephoned them again. Had Mr. Green called? He had. This was his number. He answered on the second ring. He would come right around with her case. No, please, gentleman's privilege. Very simple mistake, must be a million AGs in the world. He'd come right away.

He held the taxi. She was quite pretty, he saw to his surprise, soft and fluffy. He sort of remembered see-

26

ing her at London Airport and thinking that if she was in the taxi queue he might suggest they share. Remembering the revelations of her diary, he shuddered with relief at his escape. She was surprised to see that he looked so pleasant; she had expected him to look like a fox: sharp-featured, mean pointed little face. He looked normal and nice. She thought she remembered him on the plane up in executive class laughing with the air hostess.

"I have your case here," she said. "It's a bit disarrayed, for want of a better word. I was hunting in it to see if I could find out where you were staying."

"Yours is a little disarrayed too." He grinned. "But none of those nice garments you have fitted me, so they're all safe and sound."

They grinned at each other almost affectionately.

He looked at her for a moment. It was only eleven o'clock at night; in London that meant the evening was only starting. She was quite lovely in a round soft sort of way. . . .

She wished he didn't have to go. Maybe if she said something about why not go and let's have a bottle of wine to celebrate the found suitcases . . .

She remembered how he had described his boss as bordering on senility and how he had given chapter and verse to prove that the boss was a heavy drinker.

He remembered how she had proposed threatened suicide with attendant letters to some guy's wife, his children and his colleagues.

They shook hands, and at exactly the same moment they said to each other that they hadn't read each other's papers or anything, and at that moment they both knew that they had.

MISS VOGEL'S
VACATION

*M*iss Vogel was surprised that she had never married. Not so much upset as surprised. When she was young everyone thought Victoria Vogel would surely be one of the first in the neighborhood to walk down an aisle.

Fair-haired, soft and pretty, a great homemaker, she even made dresses for herself and her sisters and their friends, as well as baking delicious desserts for any event where good cooking was needed.

The young Miss Vogel had an agreeable manner with everyone; no future mother-in-law would stand in her way, no family would object to the girl who worked pleasantly in her father's bakery. She was much in demand to dance at the weddings of her many friends, and although she caught the bride's bouquet on many occasions, it never led to a wedding of her own.

Miss Vogel didn't look back on her girlhood in New York as a lonely time; she hadn't yearned always for a beau of her own. She always thought there was one around the next corner. She lived happily over the bakery and didn't really notice the years go by.

There were so many other things to think about. Like her mother's illness. The others were all married by the time Miss Vogel's mother took to her bed, so she did the nursing, which made sense because she lived at home.

And when her mother died and her father became gloomy and lost interest in his work, she had to work all that much harder in the bakery to keep it going. There was a manager, of course, Tony Bari. They spent long hours together trying to see how the bills could be paid, the overheads reduced, and the whole enterprise made sound.

Everyone thought one day they might marry.

Miss Vogel didn't really think they would, even though she would have been happy had their quick embraces led to a proposal.

But she was a practical woman and realized that

Tony Bari was very interested in money and had told her several times that any sensible man in business was looking for a rich wife. Miss Vogel knew she wasn't in this category, and even though she did like his company, his big broad smile and the way his mustache tickled her cheek, she didn't weep when he told her he had finally met a lady of property and invited her to his wedding.

Not long after, Miss Vogel's father went to the hospital, and it was known that he would not come out. Tony Bari bought the business. His new wife did not think it appropriate that Miss Vogel continue to work and live there, so, at the age of thirty, she was unemployed.

People said Tony Bari had not paid enough, and indeed, after it had been divided between her sisters and brothers there was very little left.

Miss Vogel had nowhere to live, she had no real qualifications to get a good job anywhere, but with her customary good humor she decided to wait until something turned up. Then she saw a position as a type of janitor or superintendent in a small, new apartment building. A lot of the residents were female, and they had specifically sought a woman super. Miss Vogel, with her calm, pleasant manner, seemed ideal, and she now had a two-room apartment, with an address in a fine part of town.

Her friends were pleased for her.

"You'll meet very classy folk now," they said.

Miss Vogel didn't mind whether they were classy or

not, just as long as they were nice. And mainly they were.

She became involved in all their lives. She walked the little yapping dog, unsuitably called Beauty, for Janet, the discontented widow in Number One.

She baby-sat for the teenage daughter of Heather, who was a workaholic advertising supremo in Number Two. She took in the flowers and arranged them for Number Three, where Francesca the attractive mistress of two businessmen lived. Tactfully, Miss Vogel made sure these two gentlemen never coincided on a visit.

She spent a lot of time in Number Four, where Marion sat and looked out the window, sad because her husband came home so rarely.

There were many others in the building whose lives were familiar to Miss Vogel. Her sisters sometimes said these must be rich, spoiled people who lacked nothing in their lives, but Miss Vogel didn't agree. As she sat in beautifully decorated apartments and drank coffee from a fine china cup or soda from cut-crystal glassware, Miss Vogel knew that unease and unhappiness didn't fly out the window just because you had money. A lot of the people had even more worries than the Vogel family ever had. Sometimes she went past the old bakery where Tony Bari had built a big business with his wife's money. It was now a delicacies shop, and people faxed in their orders for sandwiches, which were delivered to their offices. Imagine!

There were three children. Miss Vogel watched

them grow up. She would have liked to have met them properly and known them, to have been invited into the store where she, too, had lived as a child.

But Tony Bari's wife never seemed to want her around.

Miss Vogel thought this was sad. She had always been welcoming and kind to the woman who had come to live there only because of her father's dollars. But then, you couldn't make people like you if they didn't.

Her days and nights were never empty or lonely, because of all the people in the apartments. Miss Vogel did not have what anyone would call a great life of her own, but she went through all theirs, their hopes and dreams for Thanksgiving and Christmas, who would come home, where they would be invited, what they would cook. Their diets for the new year, how many days a week working out at the gym, low-fat foods to be stocked in the freezer. Then she went through their new wardrobes for spring. None seemed to notice Miss Vogel didn't buy spring clothes, plan to lose ten pounds every January, or discuss where she went for Thanksgiving or Christmas.

She was a listening person, not a talking person.

She was interested in their lives.

Now it was time to talk about vacations.

Janet was going to Arizona with her sister, so naturally there was the matter of Beauty, the bad-tempered little dog, Beauty didn't like kennels, so perhaps Miss Vogel . . .

Heather could take only a week and not one day more away from work, so she would fly to Los Angeles. This way, she could fit in one or two meetings on the West Coast as well as take fourteen-year-old Heidi to Disneyland and Universal Studios, so it would be a fantastic holiday for the child. But there was simply no time to get her any vacation clothes. Could Miss Vogel manage . . . one Saturday morning possibly? Just a quick trip to the department store?

Francesca was going to spend one week with one man and the other with the second man, but she had told each she was going to a health spa for the week she would not be with him. Would Miss Vogel mind very much taking the bus to this town two miles away, where the spa actually was, and mailing two postcards for her? You see, men were so possessive and so suspicious these days, and one didn't want to do anything silly.

Marion in Number Four was uncharacteristically cheerful because she and her husband were going to a quiet inn—he said he would like time to talk properly. That had to be good, Marion said, vacations were a time when people found new relationships if they had none or cemented an existing one that needed to be patched up.

That was the wonderful thing about vacations, wasn't it, Marion had said over and over.

Miss Vogel didn't know. She had never had a vacation. There had never been the opportunity, the money, or the time. And now, at fifty-three, there seemed little point in hoping she would find a new relationship, and there wasn't an old one to cement.

Tony Bari and his wife and children were going to Italy. Her sisters, brothers, and their families were going to a lake where they rented chalets every year. Nice for the cousins to get to know each other and keep in touch, they said.

None of them ever thought it might be nice for Miss Vogel to get to know them all and keep in touch, too. But then, she would be out of place. An elderly aunt on her own.

All the holidays seemed to come together. Miss Vogel would have a very empty building to look after. But she enthused about their trips, as she had enthused for so many years about everything they did.

She did all she was asked to do. She studied the feeding schedules of the small, aggressive Beauty to reassure Janet. She took Heidi on an outing to Bloomingdale's and with Heather's dollars bought her bright-colored clothes to wear in the California sun. She planned the two bus trips so she could send the deceiving postcards for Francesca. She helped Marion pack romantic negligees for her week in the country inn.

And, of course, she would do all the other things that made them think Miss Vogel was an angel. She would turn out their lights, pull their drapes at different times each evening, sort their mail, so, when they came back, it would be in a neat pile on their hall table. She would see their garments were returned from the dry cleaner and hung in their closets; she would admit a television repairman here and an interior decorator there and listen to their holiday tales and look at their holiday photos with great interest on their return.

Often there was fuss and near hysteria at the actual time of departure; limousines had not been ordered in advance, for example, or taxis could not be hailed on the New York streets.

This year, Miss Vogel decided to cut through all the drama and found a neighborhood car service. She spoke to Frank, a man with a tired, kind face, who was at the desk, telling him she had four trips over two days, to La Guardia Airport for Heather and Heidi, to Grand Central for Janet, to Penn Station for Marion and her husband, and some secret pickup place in New Jersey for Francesca.

"What commission are you looking for?" Frank asked wearily.

"Oh no," Miss Vogel said. "I was only trying to arrange something for the people in my building. They'll all pay you the rate. I don't want anything . . . I don't want anything for myself."

"You must be the only person in the world who doesn't, then," said Frank.

"It's just their vacations. They get very fussed, you know the way people do?"

"I don't know the way people do," Frank said. "I've never had a vacation."

38

Miss Vogel gave him a big smile. "Do you know neither have I? We must be the only people in the world who haven't."

A bond was established between them, and they worked out the times he would be there to pick up the holidaymakers.

He was courteous and punctual, but more than that he was kind. He waited while Janet kissed Beauty good-bye; he told Heidi she'd love Disneyland— everyone came back from it a new person; he explained to Francesca that he was a genius at finding out-of-the-way spots in New Jersey; he told Marion and her husband that an inn in the countryside was the very best vacation anyone could choose.

Miss Vogel was sorry when the last had gone. She enjoyed Frank's company. She would miss regular visits when she always found time to make him a coffee and give him some of her own home-baked shortbread.

To her surprise, he turned up again.

"I was wondering, Miss Vogel, if you and I should have a vacation in New York," he began tentatively. "We could pretend we were tourists here and see it through their eyes." He looked at her, hoping that she would not laugh at this or dismiss it as a ridiculous idea.

"A vacation in New York City?" she said thoughtfully.

"Well, a lot of people do, you know." Frank was defensive. "I drive them to places. I should know."

"That will be great," said Miss Vogel. "But first I have to do a bit of fussing. That's essential."

"Yes, I'll come around tomorrow morning. Does that give you time enough to fuss?" he asked.

Miss Vogel worked out that she could take a five-hour vacation each day. Then she ironed her clothes carefully and laid out a different outfit for each outing. She went to a beauty parlor on the corner and got her hair and her nails done.

She prepared several picnic lunches they could have and left them ready in the freezer. She got new heels on her comfortable shoes. She checked the weather forecast. She was ready for her vacation.

They went to Ellis Island and spent the day looking at where their grandparents had come into the United States from Italy and Germany, Ireland and Sweden.

"I bet they were four young people who never had time for a vacation once they got here," Miss Vogel said.

"But they must have been adventurous young people," Frank replied, "not the kind of folk who would like to believe their descendants would be stay-at-homes."

The next day they went to the World Trade Center to see the view and then back uptown to the zoo. Afterward, they walked in Central Park in the sunshine.

They drove together companionably to the town where they had to mail Francesca's postcards and talked about how old life was with so many people living a lie—Francesca herself and the two married men who were each taking her off for a week. They went to Chinatown and on a tour of the stock exchange on Wall Street.

They went back to where Miss Vogel grew up and looked at the big delicacies shop, so much changed in appearance since her youth. They went to see where Frank was raised, changed so very much from when he was a boy. He pointed out where he had lived with his wife for three years a long time ago, and also the hospital where she had died.

Neither had ever been to Carnegie Hall, so they booked a concert.

And as she had seen a ball game only on television, never in reality, they went to Yankee Stadium.

And the week flew by.

Frank helped Miss Vogel to sort the mail, arrange the curtains, and arrange deliveries for the tenants. Miss Vogel went to the car-service office and brightened it up by washing the curtains and putting some colorful ornaments around.

The next week, they could no longer afford five hours a day for vacation. Like everyone else in New York, they would now know that feeling which said the holiday was over.

But for Frank and Miss Vogel, there was something new and wonderful. No longer did they keep their thoughts to themselves, there was someone with whom to talk over the events of the day. Not only holiday memories, but what was happening in the real world as well.

So when Frank drove Heather and Heidi back from the airport, he could report that mother and daughter were hardly speaking and that the girl had been left alone in her hotel room looking at television, since Heather was tied up in meetings all day.

Miss Vogel could tell him that something very odd had happened in Francesca's life—perhaps both men had proposed marriage to her, both would leave their wives, but she wanted neither. Francesca was lying down with a cold compress on her eyes, trying to get the courage to tell them.

Janet told Frank in the car her holiday with her sister had been a huge mistake—there would be no more family get-togethers. What did people want family for, anyway? A good dog was worth twenty sisters.

Marion told Miss Vogel that her rat of a husband had taken her to the inn only to tell her he was leaving her. And amazingly, Marion didn't really mind all that much. Once it was out in the open, she enjoyed the walking and peace of the countryside, and her husband had been startled and annoyed at how well she adapted to the new situation.

But nobody asked Miss Vogel if she had enjoyed her time when they were away. And if they saw Frank around the place a lot, it was because they assumed he was driving people. Sometimes Miss Vogel wasn't quite as available to baby-sit, walk dogs, listen to problems, arrange flowers. Nothing you could put your finger on. And if she looked happier and walked with a spring in her step and smiled with brighter eyes . . . they thought she might have lost a few pounds or something.

Tony Bari's wife noticed, however. She had returned from a tedious vacation in Italy with a lot of possessive in-laws and was glad to be back in New York. Her eyes narrowed when Miss Vogel came into the shop. She always suspected Tony Bari harbored feelings for the daughter of the house, and if she had had any money, he would very probably have asked Miss Vogel to marry him.

"Did you have a good vacation, Miss Vogel?" she asked politely, her sharp glance taking in Miss Vogel's improved posture, hairstyle, and general manner.

"Very pleasant, Mrs. Bari. I stayed in New York, got to know my own city. It was delightful."

Tony Bari's wife, who would love to have done the same, was envious.

"Well, at our age, Miss Vogel, we don't expect very much from vacations, do we?" She was trying to remove the pleased smile from Miss Vogel's face. But she was not succeeding.

Miss Vogel paused in her choosing of expensive mushrooms, specialty cheese, and exotic olive oils and smiled confidently at the woman who had taken away her only hope of marriage and a home, merely because that woman's father had money.

"Oh, Mrs. Bari, how sad, how very sad to hear you

say that," she said, as deeply sympathetic as if she were offering condolences at a funeral.

Tony Bari was at the other side of the shop. He was fat now and balding, his face set in lines of disappointment and greed. Life had not turned out as he might have wished. How could she ever have thought he would have made her a good husband? Had it all worked out at the time, then she would have just returned from a weary journey to Italy with this bad-tempered man. She would have known no other world but this one; she would never have gone in and out of the lives of the existing people who lived in her building.

She might have looked wistfully at the kind face of Frank, a limousine driver, if she had ever met him, and wondered what it would be like to live in easy companionship with someone who saw beauty everywhere and gain and opportunity nowhere. Tonight, for his birthday, she would cook him a great feast. They had plans for the future, plans young people were making all over the world, but were no less loving and hopeful just because Miss Vogel and Frank were no longer young.

"Oh, Mrs. Bari," she repeated, her voice full of genuine sorrow. She had been about to ask, "What *is* the point of living at all if we don't expect something from every vacation and every day?" but it sounded a bit preachy, and Miss Vogel had learned firsthand from her apartment complex that happiness does not always go hand in hand with having a lot of possessions, so instead she said that to have unrealistic dreams should not be part of the aging process.

And head high, her shopping basket full of exotic ingredients, Miss Vogel left the delicacies shop that had once been her father's bakery and, without a backward glance, walked into the sun-filled streets of New York.

THE HOME SITTER

*I*t would be a new start. Not everyone got such a chance, Maura told herself. Three months in a warm climate, and the people were supposed to be very friendly over there. Already she had got letters from faculty wives welcoming her. James would be visiting lecturer in this small university in the Midwest of America. Both fares were paid and they would have a house on campus.

The only problem was their house. James and Maura lived in a part of Dublin where people suspected burglars of lurking in the well-kept shrubbery, waiting till the owners had left each day. If they were gone for three months, the place would be ransacked.

But it was quite impossible to let the place. First there was the fear that you might never get the people out. You heard such terrible stories. Then it would mean locking everything away—no, it would be intolerable. How could they enjoy three months in a faraway place terrified that everything they had was being smashed and they might have to go to the High Court to evict the tenants.

There were no possibilities, either, in their families. Ruefully they agreed that James's mother would be an unlikely starter. She was forgetful to a point where nobody could leave her in charge. The burglar alarm would be ringing night and day, making the neighbors crazy. She did love their dog Jessie, but she would forget to feed her, or else give her all the wrong things. She would allow Jessie out and there would be litters of highly unsatisfactory puppies on the way when they got back.

They couldn't ask Maura's sister Geraldine, either, because she hated dogs. She would leap in terror when Jessie gave a perfectly normal greeting. And Maura feared that Geraldine would poke around, look in drawers and things. There would be so much hiding involved, and having to send Jessie to a kennel, that it literally wouldn't be worth it.

Their neighbors weren't the kind of people you could give a key to. These were big houses with sizable gardens. Not estates, or back-to-back terraces like Coronation Street, where everyone knew everyone's business. On one side there were the Greens, elderly, mad about gardening, hardly ever out of their greenhouse. Very pleasant to greet, of course. But that was all. And then, on the other side, there were that high-flying couple, the Hurleys, who were always being written about in the papers. They had started their own company. They had three children of their own and had adopted others. They had his mother and her father living in a kind of mews. They always seemed to have at least three students of different nationalities living with them and minding the children. You couldn't ask the Hurleys to take on any more. They'd sicken you with how much they were doing already.

"I don't know *what* we're going to do," Maura heard herself say for the tenth time to James, and saw with alarm that familiar look of of irritation cross his face.

"Everything is a problem these days," he said. "Most people would jump at this opportunity. All it does for us is create more and more difficulties."

She knew that this was true. Other people would see it as an excitement, a challenge, an adventure. She was being middle-aged beyond her years to see the summer as another Bad Thing. She must pull herself together. This trip to America was probably the last chance she would have to make her marriage work. They would be together in a new place, sharing everything as they had ten years before. There would be freedom, there would be time. James wouldn't work late at the college there, as he did at home. He wouldn't stop for drinks at the club rather than coming back to her. He wouldn't invent things to do on weekends to escape the house and the prospect of yet more time mending, fixing, and titivating their home.

Maura reminded herself that she was resourceful, that that was how she had found James in the beginning, her lecturer in college whom everyone had fancied and yet Maura had won. That was how she had found the house. It was good to be hardworking and practical. That was what had saved them both when little Jamie had died, a cot death at three months. Maura had planted the garden and bought a young collie dog. James had always said that she was a tower of strength in those months.

But that had been six years ago, and things had changed a lot since then. It wasn't just the lack of a child. They both knew that. There seemed to be a gulf between them that no amount of shared interest would bridge. There were so many things that they did share already—the house, the garden, the walks with Jessie—and yet there were so many silences. Another child, even if it had come along, would not have cemented them together. James lived more and more in the college, Maura more and more in her office, which she didn't really enjoy, but since the work was routine and simple it gave her plenty of time to think about her home and its constant improvement.

There was something about the frown of impatience on James's face that made Maura realize the urgency of sorting out the house matter without any more fuss.

"Leave it to me," she said reassuringly. "I'll think of something. You have enough to do to prepare your lectures."

The frown went, and there was something of the old James. "That's more like it," he said. He was very handsome when he smiled. Maura realized with a sudden lurch of feeling that at least three marriages had ended in the college. It had been shock and horror and scandal at the time, but now all those men had settled down happily with their second choice. The furor had died down except in the hearts of the three women who had been left alone. It could happen with James very, very easily. If someone wanted him desperately enough. If Maura was foolish enough to drive him out of the home with her fussing and creating problems where none existed.

She spent the next day on the phone. Did anyone know anyone? And eventually someone did. An old school friend Maura hadn't seen for years knew someone called Allie.

"Is she an Arab?" Maura asked. The Hurleys had a boy called Ali staying one year.

"No, it's short for Alice, I think. She's a kind of a home sitter."

"Is she in an organization? Does she get paid?"

The friend, a colorless woman called Patsy, said no, Allie was a law unto herself. "She's our age, but you'd think she was years younger. She hasn't anywhere to live, no real job, she just moves on from place to place minding people's houses."

"Sounds a bit unreliable," Maura said disapprovingly.

"No, she was very good here, actually." Patsy sounded grudging.

"And what did she do all day?"

"I wish I knew, but she had the place in fine shape when we came back from Brussels. Everyone around spoke highly of her." There was still something ungiving about Patsy. Maura wondered if she was being told the full story about this Allie.

"You didn't like her, did you?" she asked.

Patsy sounded aggrieved. "Lord almighty, Maura, you asked for someone to mind your house, I found you someone. Did I like her? I hardly met her. I only saw her twice before we left, and once when we came back. She did everything she said she would, and what more can anyone ask?"

Maura thanked her hastily and took Allie's present phone number. She was minding an art gallery for someone. It would be lovely to go to a home with a dog and a garden, she said.

"And two budgies?" Maura added.

"Super," said Allie.

She sounded eighteen, not thirty-five-ish. When

they met her, she looked much nearer to eighteen also.

Allie had long, dark, curly hair, the kind you knew she shampooed every morning and just shook it dry. She had a great smile that lit up her whole face, she had long golden legs and arms, and she wore what Maura thought was an overshort denim dress.

Allie sat on the grass as she talked to them in the garden. She smiled up at James, and Maura felt a resentment that she had not known possible. Not just at the fact that Allie *could* sit on the ground without falling over. But at the way she looked at James. It wasn't flirtatious or coy, it was just a look that was full of interest. Everything he said seemed worthy of consideration; Allie would nod eagerly or shake her head. She was reacting on a very high level. Not for Allie the nods and grunts and half-attention that James must have been used to from Maura.

To be fair, and Maura struggled to be fair, Allie seemed very interested in her too. She asked Maura about her job, and even James seemed surprised at some of the things he heard about Maura's daily routine.

"I didn't know that," he said, interested, and Maura realized with a pang that she hardly ever told James anything about work nowadays except to complain about the manager or the difficulty in parking a car or getting any shopping done at lunch hour.

Allie had a big red notebook, and she wrote their names down neatly, and all contact addresses that she would need. She was practical, too, asking about plumbers and electricians, and the number to phone if she smelled gas. She asked them to be sure to put any silver in the bank and to spend a couple of hours assembling all their private papers and documents and to lock them up somewhere.

"We don't need to do that." James was smiling that slightly besotted smile men in their late thirties smile, Maura noticed.

"Oh, but you do, James." Allie was firm. "You see, I come from having minded dozens of homes; you haven't. When you are over in America you'll suddenly remember that you left something out you'd prefer that nobody else saw. This way you'll know you didn't. Also, you can't ask me to pay your dentist's bill or find your income tax for you if it's all locked away, so I'm protecting myself, too."

Allie had a marvelous laugh; she threw her head back and laughed like a child. She had perfect teeth, and her neck was long and suntanned.

Maura felt herself patting her hair. She was middle-aged, frumpish and settled, in her tights and shoes beside this lovely, leggy thing, all canvas shoes and golden limbs. And if Maura noticed it, then you could be sure that James did.

Allie asked about relations and friends, noted their names and numbers. She wrote down that Maura's sister didn't like dogs, and that James's mother didn't lock doors behind her. She seemed to understand everything in an instant.

Allie told them that she would write every week and give them an update on everything. She took instructions about phone messages and redirection of mail.

"Well, wasn't that the direct intervention of God," James said when Allie had finally left.

Maura felt that this was both going too far and also ignoring her own part in finding the home sitter.

"Yes, well, and my friend Patsy!" she said mulishly.

"Of course." He didn't care about niceties like this. "Isn't she a treasure?

"She's exactly what we want," he said happily. "I didn't dream that anyone like that existed."

A cold, hard knot formed in Maura's stomach. She felt a physical shock, like the feeling you get if you think you've swallowed a piece of glass. She realized she must not show her anxiety.

"Yes, she seems terrific, all right."

"Aren't you clever?" James said.

Maura could feel the back of her neck get cold and clammy. As she sat in her garden, she knew in a disembodied way that she would remember this moment forever. She knew the time and the date, and the way she sat on the garden seat with her hand stroking the head of Jessie the collie dog. Maura knew, with a certainty that she had never felt before about anything, that Allie was going to bring danger into her life. Real danger, threatening everything she had hoped for.

She had often wondered how women behaved once they knew for certain. But then she supposed few women were possessed of the foresight that she had.

Other women had to wait for evidence and proof, or a friend whispering that perhaps she ought to know. Or worse still, the husband saying there was something he had to tell her.

Maura wondered if it was better to know so far in advance. Did it give her any advantage over the others? Were there any points to be gained in the game of trying to keep James for herself, and resist the siren call of Allie, who had already captured his heart?

It wasn't a question of competing. Maura had thick, fine, fair hair; she couldn't grow a mop of dark curls to shake around. Her mouth was small, almost pursed; this had once been thought an advantage, but she couldn't laugh showing all those pearly teeth as Allie did. Maura's legs and arms were white, not long and golden. If it were a straight fight, Allie would have the scepter and the crown. It couldn't be a straight fight.

They saw her once more before they left—the very morning of the departure. She had brought her own sheets, she told them, and they saw them peeping from a huge straw basket.

"Is that the only luggage you have?" Maura tried hard to stop her voice from sounding like Allie's mother or her schoolteacher.

Allie dimpled back at her. "I'm a gypsy, you see. I don't need possessions. I use everybody else's. I'll watch your television, look at your clocks, listen to your radio, boil your kettle. . . . I don't need to clutter myself up with a lot of things."

James was listening to this as if it were words from

the Book of Revelations. He was also looking at the corner of Allie's sheets. Pretty blue and pink flowers with frilly edges on them. Maura knew that her own dull fitted sheets in white and pink were uninviting by comparison.

It had never been difficult to work out James's thought processes. They were very simple and direct; they went relentlessly from point A to point B.

"We never asked you, Allie, if there is anyone . . . any friend . . . boy . . . man . . ." He broke off in confusion.

"Allie knows she can invite any friend here." Maura was crisp.

"No, I meant . . . you know." James looked pathetic; he was dying to know if there was anyone. Maura held her breath, but not with any hope. What she had felt as she sat on that garden seat had not been a suspicion, it had been a foresight. It wasn't a matter of fearing that this golden girl would destroy Maura's life. She didn't just fear it, she knew it.

Allie laughed lightly. "Oh, don't worry about that, James," she said. "I'm between lovers at the moment."

"I'm sure that state won't last very long." He was being gallant, arch. Idiotic.

"You'd be surprised." The smile was easy. "I have to wait for the right man."

Maura knew that Allie would wait three months. The right man, James, was being taken out of the country temporarily, but she would wait and plot and plan for his return.

She wrote every week, addressing the letters to Maura, but this was only a ploy. She talked of long walks on the beach in Killiney throwing the sticks for Jessie, chatting with James's mother. A remarkable woman for her age, and so interesting about the year she had spent in Africa.

"Poor Mum, delighted with a new audience," James said.

Allie had contacted Maura's sister Geraldine; they had, it seemed, been visiting each other a lot. Maura hoped this didn't mean that Geraldine would be dropping in at all hours when they got back.

Geraldine had been frightened by a dog when she was young; this was where her fear stemmed from.

"I didn't know that," James said.

"Neither did I." Maura was grim.

The visit to the midwestern campus was a sort of success. Only a "sort of," Maura thought.

There was indeed a chance to get closer. Evenings on their own. Walks together. None of the pressures of home, no traffic to cope with or talk about, since they lived in the center of everything. No duty calls to people, no telephone ringing except from kind neighbors asking them to drop by for a barbecue or a drink.

But the week seemed to be spent waiting for Allie's next letter and analyzing the last one.

"Imagine, the Hurleys asked her to dinner," James said.

Maura had noted that too. "Very kind of them. They're wonderful at looking after strays," she said. It had been a mistake. James frowned.

"I don't think you'll find that they classified our Allie as a stray," he said.

Maura hated her being called "our Allie." She also hated hearing in a letter that old Mrs. Green was much better now and would be coming home from the hospital soon with a new hip.

"I didn't know . . ." James began.

"I didn't know she had a hip replacement either," Maura said. "They keep themselves very much to themselves."

"Not anymore they don't," James said tersely.

"Will we send them a card?" Maura sounded tentative.

"You were always the one afraid of drawing them on ourselves."

"Well, since they've *been* drawn . . ." She knew her voice sounded sharp.

"Up to you." He sounded a million miles away. Or a few thousand miles away. Back in that house and garden, in those flowery sheets, on warm terms with the neighbors. Maura felt that cold knot return. Like a flashback in a film, she saw herself sitting with a hand on Jessie's soft velvet fur.

There was a chill in the warm American evening, and she gave a little shiver.

"Are you all right?" he asked, concerned. He would always be kind to her, see that she managed as well as possible in the circumstances. She could see into the future, when he would call around once a year to discuss investments, and whether the roof needed to be redone.

But where would he call? She would *not* give him the house, she would not walk out and let Allie take over that place she had loved and lavished her heart on for ten years.

She would live there alone if need be. Her eyes filled with tears.

"You seem very tense here," he said kindly. "If you like, we can get away a little earlier. I mean, I can cram the lectures together a bit towards the end. Be back sooner."

"What about Allie? She thinks she is staying three months."

"Oh, she can stay on with us surely? Until she goes to her next place. She's not a fusser, our Allie."

Maura said she didn't feel a bit tense, she simply loved it here, there was no question of going home early. She knew her smile was small and pinched. Without surgery she would never have a broad, open smile like Allie's.

It was a perfect September day when they got home. Maura rang Allie from the airport.

"How did she sound?" James was eager.

Maura wanted to say that she sounded like an overgrown schoolgirl, laughing and welcoming them back and words tumbling over each other. Instead she said that Allie sounded fine, and that she had arranged a

few people to come in. "That was lovely of her."
James smiled happily. "Friends of hers, is it?"

"No, friends of ours, I think," Maura said.

"We don't have that many friends," James said absently.

"Of course we do," Maura snapped.

Around them in Dublin Airport passengers were being met, embraced, and ferried out to cars. Maura and James pushed their trolley of luggage to a taxi ungreeted.

"We *could* have been met if we had wanted it," Maura said in answer to no question.

On their lawn, Allie had set up a table. She had vases of flowers, and jugs of sangria. James's mother was there, helping and feeling as if she were in charge. Geraldine was there with her mute husband Maurice, chatting animatedly to the elderly Mr. and Mrs. Green, and discussing the success of the operation. The Hurleys were there with their extended family. The children all seemed to know Allie well. Maura had to struggle to remember their names, there were so many of them. A couple from across the road whom Maura and James had never met were among the crowd milling around.

"I do hope we aren't intruding," the woman said. "But Allie was so insistent, she said you'd love everyone here."

"She was utterly right." Maura strove to put the warmth and enthusiasm into her voice that she knew were called for.

"Have a shower, you must be exhausted." Allie had thought of everything.

Maura stood under the water while James shaved at the washbasin nearby.

"What a girl," he said at least three times. He was anxious to be back down there joining in the fun. "Wasn't this a smashing idea of hers?"

Maura's voice was shaky. "Great," she said, hoping the running water covered the sound of a sob. "Simply great. You go on down. I'll be out in a minute."

She stood in her bedroom and tried to find something that might look festive and happy to wear. She seemed to see only blouses and skirts or matronly dresses that would make her fit into the generation of James's mother or the Greens.

Allie was leaving that afternoon; she would not stay and destroy Maura's life by taking her husband. Her next job was abroad. Minding a farmhouse in the Dordogne.

But Maura had been right that day on the garden seat. Allie had ruined her life; she had opened up golden doors and shown everyone else how wonderful things could be, but would never be again. James's mother would never again be asked to tell long stories about Africa, Geraldine wouldn't be invited to tell rambling tales of self-pity about barking dogs in her youth. The old Greens would go back into their greenhouse, and the high-flying Hurleys behind their hedge.

The people who lived across the road would never intrude again. James would frown without knowing why, and only Maura would know that nothing would ever be the same.

PACKAGE TOUR

*T*hey met at a Christmas party, and suddenly every-thing looked bright and full of glitter instead of commercial and tawdry, as it had looked some minutes before.

They got on like a house on fire and afterward when they talked about it they wondered about the silly expression. "A house on fire." It really didn't mean anything, like two people getting to know each other and discovering more and more things in common. They were the same age, each of them one quarter of a century old. Shane worked in a bank, Moya worked in an insurance office. Shane was from Galway and went home every month. Moya was from Clare and went home every three weeks. Shane's mother was difficult and wanted him to be a priest. Moya's father was difficult and had to be told that she was staying in a hostel in Dublin rather than a bed-sitter.

Shane played a lot of squash because he was afraid of getting a heart attack or, worse, of getting fat and being passed over when aggressive, lean fellows were promoted. Moya went to a gym twice a week because she wanted to look like Jane Fonda when she grew old and because she wanted to have great stamina for her holidays.

They both loved foreign holidays, and on their first evening out together Shane told all about his trips to Tunisia and Yugoslavia and Sicily. In turn, Moya told her tales of Tangiers, Turkey, and of Cyprus. Alone among their friends they seemed to think that a good foreign holiday was the high spot of the year.

Moya said that most people she knew spent the money on clothes, and Shane complained that in his group it went on cars or drink. They were soul mates who had met over warm, sparkling wine at a Christmas party where neither of them knew anyone else. It had been written for them in the stars.

When the January brochures came out, Moya and

Shane were the first to collect them; they had plastic bags full of them before anyone else had got around to thinking of a holiday. They noted which were the bargains, where were early-season or late-season three-for-the-price-of-two-week holidays. They worked out the jargon.

Attractive flowers cascading down from galleries could mean the place was alive with mosquitoes. Panoramic views of the harbor might mean the hotel was up an unmerciful hill. *Simple* might mean no plumbing, and *sophisticated* could suggest all-night discos.

The thing they felt most bitter about was the single-room supplement. It was outrageous to penalize people for being individuals. Why should travel companies expect that people go off on their holidays two by two like the animals into an ark? And how was it that the general public obeyed them so slavishly? Moya could tell you of people who went on trips with others simply on the basis that they all got their holidays in the first fortnight in June.

Shane said that he knew fellows who went to Spain as friends and came home as enemies because their outing had been on the very same basis. Timing.

But as the months went on and the meetings became more frequent and the choice of holiday that each of them would settle for was gradually narrowed down, they began to realize that this summer they would probably travel together. That it was silly to put off this realization. They had better admit it.

They admitted it easily one evening over a plate of spaghetti.

It had been down to two choices now. The Italian lakes or the island of Crete. And somehow it came to both of them at the same time: This would be the year they would go to Crete. The only knotty problem was the matter of the single room.

They were not as yet lovers. They didn't want to be rushed into it by the expediency of a double booking. They didn't want it to be put off-limits by the fact of having booked two separate rooms. Shane said that perhaps the most sensible thing would be to book a room with two beds. This had to be stipulated on the booking form. A twin-bedded room. Not a double bed.

Shane and Moya assured each other they were grown-ups.

They could sleep easily in two separate beds, and suppose, just suppose in the fullness of time after mature consideration and based on an equal decision with no one party forcing the other . . . they wanted to sleep in the same bed . . . then the facility, however narrow, would be there for them.

They congratulated each other on their maturity and paid the booking deposit. They had agreed on a middle-of-the-road kind of hotel, in one of the resorts that had not yet been totally discovered and destroyed. They had picked June, which they thought would avoid the worst crowds. They each had a savings plan. They knew that this year was going to be the best year in their lives and the holiday would be the first of many taken together all over the world.

The cloud didn't come over the horizon until March when they were sitting companionably reading a glossy magazine. Shane pointed out a huge suitcase on wheels with a matching smaller suitcase. Weren't they smashing, he said; a bit pricey, but maybe it would be worth it.

Moya thought she must be looking at the wrong page. Those were the kind of suitcases that Americans bought for going around the world.

Shane thought that Moya couldn't be looking at the right page; they were just two normal suitcases, but smart and easy to identify on the carousel. Just right for a two-week holiday. But for how many people? Moya wondered wildly; surely the two of them wouldn't have enough to fill even the smaller suitcase. Well for one person, me, Shane said with a puzzled look.

Between the two happy young people there was a sudden gray area. Up to now their relationship had been so open and free, but suddenly there were unspoken things hovering in the air. They had told each other that their friends' romances had failed and even their marriages had rocked because they had never been able to clear the air. Shane and Moya would not be like that. But still, neither one of them seemed able to bring up the subject of the suitcases. The gulf between them was huge.

Yet in other ways they seemed just as happy as before. They went for walks along the pier, they played their squash and went to the gym, they enjoyed each other's friends, and both of them managed to put the disturbing black cloud about the luggage into the background of their minds. Until April, when another storm came and settled on them.

It was Moya's birthday, and she unwrapped her gift from Shane, which was a traveling iron. She turned it around and around and examined it in case it was something else disguised as a traveling iron. In the *hope* that it was something disguised as a traveling iron. But no, that's what it was.

It was lovely, she said faintly.

Shane said he knew ladies loved to have something to take the creases out on holidays, and perhaps Moya shouldn't throw away the tissue paper; it was terrific for folding into clothes when you were packing, it took out all that crumpled look, didn't she find?

Moya sat down very suddenly. Absolutely on a different subject, she said she wondered how many shirts Shane took on holiday. Well, fifteen obviously, and the one he was wearing and sports shirts and a couple of beach shirts.

"Twenty shirts?" Moya said faintly.

That was about it.

And would there be twenty socks and knickers, too? Well, give or take. Give or take how many? A pair or two. There seemed to be a selection of shoes and belts, and the odd sun hat.

Moya felt all the time that Shane would smile his

lovely familiar, heart-turning smile and say, "I had you fooled, hadn't I?" and they would fall happily into each other's arms. But Shane said nothing.

Shane was hoping that Moya would tell him soon where all this list of faintly haranguing questions was leading. Why she was asking him in such a robotic voice about perfectly normal things. It was as if she asked him did he brush his teeth or did he put on his clothes before leaving the house. He stared at her anxiously. Perhaps he wasn't showing enough interest in her wardrobe? Maybe he should ask about her gear.

That did not seem to be a happy solution. Moya, it turned out, was a person who had never checked in a suitcase in her life; she had a soft squelchy bag of the exact proportions that would fit under an airline seat and would pass as carry-on baggage. She brought three knickers, three bras, three shirts, three skirts, and three bathing suits. She brought a sponge bag, a pair of flip-flop sandals, and a small tube of travel detergent.

She thought that a holiday should never involve waiting for your bags at any airport, and never take in dressing for dinner, and the idea of carrying home laundry bags of dirty clothes was as foreign to her as it was to Shane—that anyone would spend holiday time washing things and drying them.

"But it only takes a minute," pleaded Moya.

"But it takes no time at all if you bring spares," pleaded Shane. "The arms would come out of your sockets carrying that lot," said Moya. "We wouldn't get into the bathroom with all your clothes draped around it," said Shane.

They talked about it very reasonably, as they had always promised each other they would do. But the rainbows had gone, and the glitter had dimmed.

It would have been better if they had actually met on holidays, they said, with Moya carrying the shabby holdall and Shane the handsome and excessive luggage. Then they would have known from the start that they weren't people who had the same views about a package tour and how you packed for it. It was a hurdle they might have crossed before they fell in love. Not a horrible shock at the height of romance.

They were practical, Moya and Shane; they wondered if it would iron itself out if they paid the single-room supplement. That way Moya wouldn't see the offending Sultan's Wardrobe, as she kept calling it, and Shane wouldn't be blinded by wet underwear, as he kept fearing. But no, it went deeper than that. It seemed to show the kind of people they were: too vastly different ever to spend two weeks, let alone a lifetime, together.

As the good practical friends they were, they went back to the travel agency and transferred their bookings to separate holidays with separate hopes and dreams.

THE
APPRENTICESHIP

*I*t was to be one of the most stylish weddings of the year. Florrie thought that if anyone had been giving odds a quarter of a century ago when she was born whether this child would ever be a guest at something like this, those odds would have been enormous. A child born in a small house in a small street in Wigan didn't seem likely to end up as the bride's best friend at what the newspapers were calling the wedding of the decade. If only her mother had lived, Florrie thought, if only her father had cared. They might have been able to get some mileage out of it, some reward for the long hours of work, the high hopes.

There would be pictures of Florrie in tomorrow's papers, probably a glimpse of her on tonight's television news. She would figure certainly in the glossy magazines, her hat alone would ensure she was well snapped. She would be seen laughing and sharing a joke, probably with some youngish and handsome member of the aristocracy. This would not be hard, because unusually for a society wedding there might not be many young women friends of the bride around. And the groom's friends, being horsey, would not be as photogenic. No, Florrie knew that she would figure in the *Tatler* and *Harper's*. And she knew how to smile without showing a mouthful of teeth and how to raise her chin in a way that made her neck look long and upper class.

She knew that it looked much more classy not to be seen with a glass in her hand, but to appear fascinated by the particular braying chap that she was meant to be talking to.

Florrie knew all of this because she had worked at it, and learned it. Like she had never worked at anything when she was at school. Long ago in a different place and at a different time, with Camilla, except of course that Camilla had not been Camilla then, she had been Ruby. And Ruby and Florrie had been best friends. As in many ways they were still best friends today. The society columns might well describe Florrie tomorrow as a very close friend of the bride. But it would not say that they had grown up together, that they had shared great doorstep sandwiches in their lunch hour, that they had collected old newspapers just so that they could read the society pages and see how people lived in a different and better world.

They had read their subject carefully, young Ruby and young Florrie. No hint of social climbing or being a hanger-on. Not even the most suspicious could fault Camilla or catch her out in a lie today. Camilla had always said she was from way up north, that her parents were dead, that she had hardly any family. Better to stick as close to the truth as possible, she had advised Florrie, less for them to unearth, and you can never be caught out in a lie. Even if they found out she had once been Ruby, Camilla was prepared to say it had been a pet name. She thought it was terribly brave and funny of Florrie to hold on to her name. But then, Florrie was such a character! Florrie had held on to her name because she remembered her mother holding her as a little girl.

"I had a doll once called Florrie," her mother had said. "I never thought I'd have a little baby of my own, a beautiful baby to look after." Florrie was three when she heard this first, hardly a baby, and still further from babyhood when her mother dressed her for school and held her face gently between red rough hands. "Florrie," she had breathed in a voice full of admiration and love. "Such a beautiful name for a beautiful little girl. They wanted me to call you Caroline . . . but I wanted a beautiful name for you, one you'd love . . . Florence. It means a flower, little Florrie, beautiful little flower."

Ruby's mother might have thought she was a little jewel. She might even have said so, but Camilla never said it. Camilla said nothing about her parents. Except that they were dead. Which was true.

They had died together in a coach crash, on the very first holiday of their married life. Florrie's father had said that's what you got for grand ideas, coach tours to the Continent, no less. Florrie's mother had said maybe they should take in the child. Ruby was eleven, and she had nobody else. Everyone had said it was a great idea. After all, it was unusual to be an only child in their street. Now Ruby and Florrie were like twins. And apart from reading all those "silly books," as people called the magazines they read, they were sensible girls, too. Not silly like some, not getting into trouble with boys. Hardworking. On Saturdays they worked in the beauty salon, and they learned how it was all done. The proprietor never had two such willing assistants. As well as sweeping floors and folding towels, they stood entranced watching the facials and manicures.

The customers liked them, two bright youngsters full of unqualified admiration. The customers didn't know they had come to learn—as they went to the fashion stores to learn, and as they worked in the good hotel to watch. And they did secretarial courses at night. By the time they had their O levels they were ready for anything. Ruby was ready to leave, to go south to start Stage Two. Florrie could go nowhere, her mother was failing fast.

She sat by her mother's bed and listened to the homespun wisdom, with a heart that was filled with impatience as well as love. She heard her mother beg her to believe that Dad was a good man really. It was just that he was a bit mulish, and drank a little too much. Dad had said no kind word in the seventeen years that Florrie had lived in his house. She nodded and pretended that she agreed with the mother, who would not be leaving hospital and coming home. Her mother said that Ruby was right to have gone to London, she was impatient, she would have been silly to stay around. The woman found nothing odd that the child she had taken in had abandoned her. Ruby has great unhappiness in her soul, she said. Florrie sat by the bed and gritted her teeth. Patience and forgiveness like this were unrealistic. Surely they couldn't be considered virtues. The nurses liked her, the handsome tall girl, a blonde with well-cut hair and long pink fingernails, unlike her stooped and work-weary mother. The daughter had character, the nurses told each other. She wouldn't stay long with the bad-tempered father once the poor woman passed away.

Florrie stayed a week. Her father's farewell was grudging, as every other gesture had been. He had always known she would go, he said, too high and mighty by far for them. No, she needn't keep coming back up, there wasn't all that much more to say.

Florrie was astonished at the change in her friend in ten short months. Vowel sounds had altered, and that wasn't all. Ruby was no longer Ruby. It's only a name, she had explained, it could have been anything.

"I know," Florrie had said. "I should have been Caroline."

"Then BE Caroline," Camilla had begged.

"Never." Florrie's eyes had flashed at the thought. They looked at each other then, a long look.

"It's only the name," Florrie had said eventually. "I'm on for everything else."

And it was like the old days. They laughed as they heard each other's phrases; you never said you had been to the WC or the toilet, it was the lavatory. You didn't say serviette, you said napkin, and it wasn't posh to have paper ones that you could throw away when they got crumpled. They had plenty of time: It was an apprenticeship, they told each other. They had until they were twenty, then they would be ready. To move among the smart and the beautiful, to be at ease among them, to marry them and live in comfort for the rest of their lives.

It would only be hard if they were unprepared. They had heard too many tales of people being trapped by their humble origins. Camilla and Florrie would be different. They would invent no pedigree that could be checked and found faulty. They would shrug and ask did such things matter anymore. They

84

would look so much the part and seem to care so little about proving themselves that soon they would be accepted. They would try hard but would never be seen to try at all; that was the secret.

And soon they were indeed ready. And it wasn't nearly as difficult as they thought. There was a career structure. Chalet girls in ski resorts, a few weeks working in smart jewelers and in art houses so that they met the right type of girl. They were slow to take up with the right type of men at the beginning. They wanted other girls to be their allies at the start. And anyway they wanted to be ready when they found the really right men. They had noticed that it wasn't only the Royals who liked their girlfriends not to have played the field; a lot of the Uppers thought that girls who had been around a lot might not be good wife material, and after all, one wouldn't like to think that lots of chaps had been with one's wife. What?

And in the meantime, because they *were* so bright and met so many people, they actually got good jobs. Camilla was high up in an estate agency and Florrie was now a partner in a firm of interior decorators. Years of watching for quality and trying to define it had paid off for both of them.

And then Camilla showed a couple of town houses to a chap who thought she was quite super and asked her to his place in the country for the weekend. She went, but she was slower than he thought to begin with a teeny affair, as he called it. In fact, she was adamant about not beginning it. He complained about her bitterly over a bottle of Bollinger to his friend Albert. Albert said that it was very rum, the girl must be mad. He'd like to meet her; he always liked meeting mad people.

Albert was of blood so blue that it almost frightened Camilla off. But she decided to take him on. This was the challenge she had spent years rehearsing for. This was the prize she had hardly dared to hope for.

Albert was intrigued by her. The girl who hadn't been to bed with his friend, who wouldn't go to bed with him either. Who wasn't frightened of his mother, who was casual to the point of indifference about her own background. She was not a gold digger, she had a position of importance in her firm. Nobody could see the potential like Camilla, they said. She dressed well, she seemed to have lots of girlfriends who all spoke glowingly of her. She had no past.

Camilla played it beautifully. She waited until Albert was truly besotted and at that precise moment she told him she was thinking of moving to Washington, D.C. There had been interest and offers; she was vague lest he ask her what interest and which offers. But she had timed it right. Albert couldn't let her leave. Albert's father predictably said she was a fine-looking filly but had she any breeding; his mother unpredictably said she was about the only kind of woman who might make a success of Albert and the rolling acres, and the complicated property investments and the tied cottages. The wedding of the decade was on.

It was decided between them that Florrie should not be the bridesmaid; the press would be too inquisitive, would ask about their origins. Papers nowadays did horrible things. They might send a photographer up to that small street and, perish the thought, find Florrie's father, surly in his suspenders. And he might tell that Camilla was Ruby and that her parents had been killed on their first coach tour abroad.

Better to have six flower girls and Albert's horsey-looking sister. Wiser to have the lovely Florrie stand out among the guests. A young woman of elegance, successful in her field. Further proof, if any were needed, that the bride was the right stuff or as right as you can get in these days of social change and upheaval.

Florrie stood in the old church and looked up at the flags of the regiment that Albert's family had fought in. The stained-glass windows remembered various ancestors, and the pews had brass plates recalling the family. The bishop was old and genial. He spoke of duty and of hope. Florrie listened as she looked at Camilla's beautiful face; she knew that her friend was listening, too.

Then the bishop spoke of love. He told how it conquered everything and that it cast out envy and ambition and greed. His eyes became misty when he talked of love.

The night before, Florrie and Camilla had talked

for a long time. They had talked as they had never been able to talk since that day when Florrie had come to London and said she would change everything, everything but her name. They laughed as they hadn't laughed for years, they drank champagne instead of the lemon tea they had learned to like when they were fourteen because they had read it was lower class to take milk.

They had said that the battle had been half won, and now that Camilla was in, she could have the right kind of dinner parties and house parties to launch her friend. Her talented friend with the wonderfully funny name. They had embraced and congratulated each other on their magical apprenticeship.

But they hadn't talked about love. And in the church where Albert's bones would lie one day, very probably beside the bones of her friend Ruby, Florrie shivered. She knew that as far as she was concerned the apprenticeship was over. She had got far enough. Perhaps she had got much farther than her friend who would appear in tomorrow's papers as the bride of the decade, who would be called Lady Camilla, who would live a life without love. They said that young girls' heads were meant to be filled with stories of love, but that had never happened to Ruby or Florrie. There had been no room in their heads, the space was too filled with rule books on how to behave and how to say "glad to know you" rather than "pleased to meet you." It had been too busy an apprenticeship to allow for thoughts of love.

Florrie would make time for it, she thought. She would not list the likely dinner guests that she might trap at her friend's long table, smiling at them confidently through Albert's family silver. When a bishop or vicar or a registrar came to say the word for Florrie, the word *love* wouldn't have an alien ring to it.

She felt somehow that the mother who had thought of her as a flower would have been pleased with her, and she was aware of tears beginning to well up in her eyes. But she willed them back, because the upper classes do not cry at christenings, weddings, or funerals. It is, after all, what sets them apart. Her apprenticeship had not been wasted.

THE BUSINESS TRIP

*L*ena had loved him for four long years. Not that he knew, of course. Men like Shay wouldn't even consider that they could be loved silently and unselfishly like that. It didn't make sense.

He probably assumed that Lena was fond of him, admired him, and might under the right circumstances be attracted to him. But if he thought of her at all, he might have assumed that she had a private life of her own. He would never have thought that this quiet, efficient assistant of his spent her entire life, both in and out of the office, thinking about him, trying to make his life easier and better, and in her dreams trying to share that life with him.

According to Maggie, Lena was not in love. She was suffering from an obsession, an infatuation. It wasn't healthy for someone who was twenty-six to develop this kind of crush on a man who didn't return it and wasn't even aware of it. And however unwise it might have been to have allowed a temporary fascination to take over, it was positively dangerous to let it continue the way Lena had. She stopped being twenty-six and became twenty-seven, and twenty-eight and twenty-nine. Soon she would be thirty years of age, and what had she to show for it?

Lena said spiritedly that she had as much to show for it as anyone had to show for anything. She had been happy, she had made his life better. She hadn't made a public fool of herself, as so many women had. She hadn't settled for second best, as so many others had done. She loved every second of her working day, which was more than you could say for a lot of people. She was appreciated if not loved in her office, and only Maggie knew her secret. She was not an object of pity. Maggie wouldn't tut-tut and shake her head over coffee with the girls about Lena's foolishness. Maggie was an ally, even if she didn't understand.

Maggie was Lena's aunt. But they had always been much more like cousins or sisters. Only ten years divided them in age, and the teenage Maggie had loved the toddler, Lena, and treated her as a friend. Now Maggie, almost forty, with huge dark eyes and a great mane of black curly hair, looked and acted younger than her niece. Her life was fuller by far. Maggie's problem had never been making men love her. It had been trying to stop them from loving her unwisely. And sometimes trying to stop herself from loving them in return—equally unwisely.

She had been married twice, widowed the first time, separated the second time, but these were only small milestones in the list of Maggie's love: Sensible married men, fathers of large and settled families, wanted to throw up everything and move in with Maggie. She often had great trouble persuading them to do nothing of the sort. It wasn't that she gave them unmentionable sexual favors, she told Lena with her big dark eyes full of honesty, it was just that they saw, however foolishly, a kind of life with her where they wouldn't be hassled and troubled. They saw a strange and unrealistic freedom in living with Maggie, something they didn't have at home. Maggie would never ask them to come to the supermarket and push the trolley, Maggie wasn't a one for wanting the grass cut or the house painted, the car cleaned or the patio built up to impress the neighbors. Maggie would be happy to eat a meal of wild mushrooms and brown bread followed by strawberries. Very far from real life. Maggie would agree with them fervently that she was indeed far from real life and they must see her only now and then. The more she protested, the more they wanted her. Lena said she was outraged at the way Maggie got every man she wanted, and yet she, Lena, who kept all the rules, couldn't get just the one.

Lena did keep the rules as written in the women's magazines. She had shiny, well-cut hair, she was tall and slim, she had been to makeup lessons to make the most of her good complexion, her fair skin, and blue eyes. She dressed well and kept her clothes immaculately. Well, why wouldn't she, Maggie grumbled, if she stayed at home every evening dreaming of lover boy Shay. There was all the time in the world to iron her blouses and sponge her skirts and polish her shoes, handbags, and belts till they shone. But had it done one bit of good in the department where she wanted it to succeed? No. None at all.

Lena's friends and colleagues all said she looked very smart, but their praise and admiration was of no interest to her. Sometimes they wondered why she didn't have a man in her life. She put them off with a laugh. And apart from Maggie, nobody had an inkling.

Maggie's grumbling had always been good-natured. But now it was different. Two things were coming up: Lena's thirtieth birthday, and a business trip with the famous Shay. Yes, he had asked the loyal Lena to London with him. Driving in his car, for a whole week.

Maggie felt it was time to play the heavy aunt for the first time in her life. She sat Lena down and told her to get ready for a serious lecture.

"Oh, not now," Lena had cried. "Not now. There's so much to be done, so many preparations. I have to decide what to wear, what to say, what social plans to set up, as well as all his business meetings. Can't the lecture wait till I get home?"

"No, it can't." Maggie was adamant. "It's about the trip; this has to be the make-or-break time. When you come back on the ferry and drive off the ramp, Shay must either be involved with you properly or else you will have given up all notion of him."

Lena's blue eyes filled with tears. "I don't want anything as definite, as black-and-white, as that. Why does it all have to hinge on this trip?" She looked appalled at having to abandon what was after all the central part of her life.

"Because you are leaving your twenties and for the first time you are leaving the country with this beauty, and you have the rest of your life ahead of you."

"It's too frightening. I don't want to try and seduce him or something like that." Lena was trembling at the thought.

"Well, what's all the fuss about what you're going to wear and how you're going to look? If you don't want him to fancy you, why don't you just go in an old sweater and a pair of jeans?" Maggie was ruthless.

"It's different for you, you can make anyone fancy you."

"So could you if you bothered. It's got nothing to do with well-cut jackets and applying your blusher properly," Maggie said.

"How, then?" Lena was eager.

"I'll tell you, but only if you promise me that you will decide one way or another at the end of the week. When you come back off that car ferry, you'll either be involved with him properly as two normal people who love each other, or you will leave that job, and put him out of your mind and heart."

"It's like doing a deal with the devil," Lena complained.

"Much more like a guardian angel," Maggie said.

They sat for three hours, Maggie with her notebook. At no stage were outfits or perfumes mentioned. There was no strategy about booking one room by mistake instead of two. There was to be no research into romantic restaurants in London where the lights would be low and there might even be violins in the background. No, if Lena was to get her man these kinds of cheap tricks were only Mickey Mouse efforts, according to Maggie. And since almost every man who moved in Dublin seemed to fancy Maggie in some way or other, she was worth listening to.

Maggie seemed shocked that Lena had worked for this man for four years, not to mention thinking that she had loved him for this length of time, and still knew so little about him. Maggie asked a string of questions. Lena knew nothing about his schooldays, whether he had liked it there or not, and how he had got into the business world in the first place. She didn't know who his first employers had been, whether he had found it easy or frightening. She didn't know what television programs he watched, and when he went to a match if it was because he knew all about the game or because he liked the sociability of it. Lena didn't know how he got on with his two brothers and sister, how often he went to see his mother. She didn't know if he liked being with his nephews and nieces. If he felt lonely on weekends, as so many people did in Dublin. How he decided what to eat and whether he had a washing machine or went to the launderette.

"What *do* you know about him, for heaven's sake?" Maggie asked with some impatience.

Lena knew all about his current and past girlfriends, and she knew the restaurants he went to, and the nightclubs, and the bills for bouquets of flowers. She knew that and she knew about him at work, where he was tough and not afraid to go into a meeting and fight.

"Well-briefed by you, of course, with reports you have been working on all weekend when you weren't putting more henna in your hair, hoping he'd notice."

"I love him," protested Lena.

"No, you don't love him at all. You don't know the first thing about him apart from this empty social thing. You might love him when you get to know him, and he might love you. But you might find him empty."

Lena refused to accept this but agreed meekly to follow Maggie's advice. In the ship's dining room over a meal she would begin, and in the long drive across Britain she would not veer between business talk and gossip-column chat about nightclubs she didn't even know. She would talk to him about himself.

"Suppose he asks me about myself?" Lena asked fearfully.

Maggie didn't much think he would, but if he did, then she was to tell him the truth. Say she was perfectly happy, she had no wish to change from her life the way it was, assure him it was satisfactory. There was nothing that drove men as mad as that—the thought that women were actually contented the way they were, not scheming and conniving.

"But that's not strictly true. I'm not totally contented the way I am," Lena complained.

Maggie shrugged. "You always tell me you are when I try to change you."

It was unanswerable.

The day before the trip Maggie rang her to wish her luck. "One thing, Lena, and remember this: He will notice you, he will fancy you. Truthfully, but you may not fancy him."

"I probably gave you much too shallow a view of him," Lena whispered in case anyone in the office would hear.

"If that was your view of him after four years of loving him, then I'm sure what you told me was very accurate," Maggie said.

Lena learned a lot that night at dinner on board

ship. She learned that his mother was demanding and never satisfied, that his brothers were discontented and jealous of his success. She heard that Shay's sisters didn't know how to bring up their children properly and gave in to them in everything. She heard that his school was full of sadistic teachers and moronic pupils, that they had ripped him off in his first job and cheated him in his second, and he had seen them coming in his third. He liked to cook but not to wash up; he thought these service apartments he lived in were a bit cramped, but he didn't want to take on the whole palaver of gardens and roofs and drains in a house. He was probably looking for something like a town house.

In the old days, like every day up to this, Lena would have immediately said she would make inquiries about town houses, and go to endless trouble ringing up auctioneers and estate agents. This time she made no offers.

"What about your house or flat, is it what you want?" he asked, almost cursorily, as if he had felt that he might have been talking just a little too much about himself.

"Oh, it's fine. I'm very happy there," she said. She told him it was a garden flat and had plenty of light as well as nice shrubs and bushes outside big windows. He nodded briskly but seemed to look at her with slightly more interest.

On the long drive to London, they talked about friends. Shay said that he ran with a very lively crowd.

No, they weren't around on weekends much, but then, he often came into the office on Saturday afternoons to do a little catching up. Lena knew this only too well. She had to cope with the results of it on Mondays: confused notes, complicated questions. She had begun every week for as long as she could remember by sorting out his thoughts for a secretary to type up. He had got all the credit. Somehow it was disappointing to know he came in only because he was bored on Saturday afternoons. She had thought it was ambition.

He took his washing to his mother, it turned out. She could not believe it, but it was true. He had to go and see the woman once a week anyway, and she had a machine, so it made sense to leave her one load and collect another. And she liked it; what else had she to do?

By the time the signposts saying Central London came up, Lena had opened more doors than she might have wished to in Shay's life.

He suggested they grab something to eat, and she said thank you but no. She had friends to see in London, so unless there was anything they wanted to discuss about work for the conference tomorrow, she would leave him to his own devices.

He seemed quite put out by this. Lena looked at his handsome face scowling with almost childlike disappointment.

"Don't tell me you're going to do the clubland circuit in London?" he asked, not very kindly.

"Lord no, that's not my world at all. Just dinner with friends."

It was true. Dinner with two old school friends— one a nun, one a nurse. They laughed and talked over old times. Something was lighter in Lena's laugh; she felt it wasn't an effort.

Next day they worked companionably at the conference, but she excused herself at lunchtime to sneak in a little shopping and said that she had a theater date in the evening. He was thoroughly bad-tempered on the second day of the conference.

"Are you going to keep running away all the time, or will we see each other at all?" he grumbled.

Big blue eyes wide, she said that honestly she was sorry . . . but since they never went out socially at home, she assumed it would be the same here. But, of course, she would be delighted to have dinner with him if he had anywhere in mind.

"I thought you might arrange somewhere," he said.

"Oh no, I wouldn't dream of it. If you are asking me to dinner, then you must, of course, choose where."

It would once have been her wildest dream. Not only was the place expensive and romantic, but as he told her tale after tale of being misunderstood, betrayed, cheated, having got even, he took her hand.

"You're very easy to talk to, Lena, and you look very lovely. I hadn't realized." She had smiled. It was a smile of someone who had known that this was predictable, not of someone who thought it was perfect.

When the evening ended and he suggested a brandy in his room, she said no. Perhaps she would prefer to have the nightcap in her room, he suggested, probably thinking that this was the height of sensitivity. No nightcap at all, Lena said. She who had planned this night for so long, and all it would lead to.

At one stage she began to wonder if Maggie had set her up. Every single harmless question she had asked had brought such a negative response that she had managed to strip Shay the man she had loved for years of any lovable quality. It was as if Maggie had known the answers in advance.

Maggie hadn't suggested that Lena talk to Shay of love.

But that night she did. They were in a restaurant looking out on the river, and he told her that he thought he loved her—yes, strange as it might seem, and having worked together for so long—but he did think he loved her.

She looked at him for a long time.

"Well, say something," he said petulantly.

"I don't have any words," she said truthfully.

He reached for her hands, but she pulled them away.

"What are you thinking about?" she asked him.

"How nice it is to love you, how there you were under my nose all the time."

At least, she thought, at least he is honest in a childish sort of way. It must be nice for him to think he's found a ready-made love under his nose, as he put it.

For years she had seen how suitable she would be for him, how right as a companion, a friend, a wife. How much she would help his career and cope with his weaknesses.

Until tonight she had never seen what it would be like for her. A lifetime of putting up with his moods, building him up when he was low, lying for him, pretending for him. And turning a blind eye when he wanted to run with a lively crowd and do the clubs and walk the blondes.

She smiled at him affectionately. It was the way she had seen her aunt Maggie smile at a multitude of men.

"What are *you* thinking about?" he asked. He was sulking now; his declaration of love had not only not been returned, it had been smiled at, patted down, soothed away.

"I was thinking about going home, about driving out of the ferry and going home," she said.

This was a very puzzling response. "Why, what will you do then?" he was anxious to know.

Lena wondered what would she do. She wouldn't leave her job just because he had said he loved her and she wouldn't love him back. She liked her work, she would stay there and overtake him if necessary. She would not fight with him or explain or apologize— Maggie never did that. She was happy in her garden flat, and now she was free as well. If some man came along—as men came along for Maggie—that she really did like, then she was free to love him.

"What will I do?" she answered him almost dreamily. The world was so full of possibilities now that the question was hard to answer. "What will I do when I get home? I think I'll telephone my aunt."

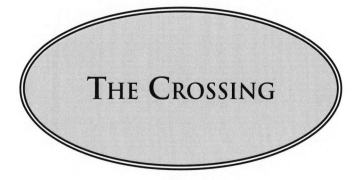

THE CROSSING

"*I*t's like a real cruise, isn't it?" Mary said, then wished she hadn't said it. What did she know about a real cruise except reading the brochures?

"I was just thinking that too," said Lavender, the older woman. "Not that I was ever on a cruise, mind, but it feels like as if we should have two weeks, and visit exotic places every day instead of just getting out at Liverpool." They laughed, united in never having been on a luxury cruise liner, united in admiring the seagulls, and valuing a few minutes away from the family.

"Are you going or coming back?" Lavender asked. She had a kind face and bright, interested eyes. Mary felt you could talk and she really might care what you said.

"Going over. The children have never seen their grandparents. It's a bit of an ordeal really."

Why had she told that to a stranger? She hadn't told any of her neighbors, nor her best friend Kath, nor her sister Betty. Why did she blurt it out to a woman with a North of England accent on the B & I boat?

"Oh, I know," Lavender consoled her. "It's always an ordeal, isn't it? Maybe we should have to live with our in-laws all the time in the same tribe and never move, or else we should never see them at all. It's the in-between bit that causes all the guilt."

This was so exactly true that Mary almost jumped to hear her own feelings echoed. . . .

"Did you have that kind of . . . well, that kind of thing, you know, with your husband's parents? Wanting to make it all closer and then getting it a bit wrong?"

"Tell me," Lavender said.

And Mary did. Every bit of it. Slowly, hesitating sometimes, going back over bits in case they hadn't been fair. How she met John when he was on a cycling holiday in Ireland. John was unhappy at college, he found it was hurting him inside his head, the stress and the worry. It wasn't only exams and study. He didn't think he would ever be happy as a teacher. He was too anxious in the classroom practice, he wouldn't be able to keep control, and he could not look forward to a life that would be a constant battle and a series of confrontations in the classroom every day.

"Why don't you do something else with your life, then?" Mary had asked him. "We only get to come onto the earth once. Wouldn't it be a pity to spend it all doing something that makes you unsettled?"

It was like a revelation to John. There and then he decided to abandon the idea of being a teacher. He wrote to the college, he wrote to his parents and to his girlfriend in London. He said he had been feeling a bit lost; now he was going to find himself in Ireland. He was going to work on a farm while he was finding out what to do with the rest of his life.

Nobody was pleased—not the college, which worried about his grant, not his girlfriend in London, who worried for four weeks and then sent a card telling him it couldn't matter less whether he found himself or didn't, since she had found somebody more normal. And his parents worried most of all. He was an only child; they had their hopes set on his being a teacher, and now he was a farmhand in Ireland, for heaven's sake. They were very disapproving. They were not people who wrote letters much or made cross-Channel phone calls. But they disapproved nonetheless. Heavily.

And when John and Mary got engaged, they assumed that it was a shotgun marriage, which it wasn't, and that it would be in a Roman Catholic Church full of images of saints and the Virgin, which it was. And they said they couldn't come to the wedding.

Mary sent pictures of the children, Jacinta, now eight, and John Paul, who was born the day the Pope came to Ireland and was seven. Looking back on it, Mary wondered if she should have chosen different names for the children. But surely that wasn't important. John's parents could hardly disapprove of a child's name as being from a different tribe. And Mary had been careful to send pictures of the children at Christmas rather than the First Communion snapshot that she felt the instinct to send each time.

Lavender was full of praise. Mary had done more than her share. And where was the problem?

It wasn't exactly a problem; there was no out-and-out war, just a distance in every sense of the word. And a dread of meeting these people, who wouldn't come to Ireland, who had never shown any greater interest than a dutiful card at Christmastime. Mary was not looking forward to hearing what a brilliant career had been cut short when John had met her in Ireland ten long years ago.

She didn't want to make excuses for the life they led in a small country town where John worked happily on a farm and Mary was a dressmaker.

And they were going now because John's father was unemployed, had been for a year, and the word had trickled back from a woman neighbor that John's dad was taking it hard. Mary had suggested they visit Ireland and as usual it had been turned down, so, gritting her teeth, she had then suggested that they take the children to visit their grandparents, and this had been agreed to. Ungraciously, of course. "You'll have to take us as you find us." But still agreed.

It was a two-week visit. Too long, Mary thought, but it was a huge undertaking, four of them to go to London; it would be a great waste to go for less time.

Lavender said that Mary was a positive gem among women. She said she was sure that the parents-in-law would be so pleased that in a few days they would all wonder whether the distance could possibly have been in their imaginations.

"Would you like a little advice?" she asked, almost shyly.

"Oh, I'd love anything you could tell me, you being English and a bit older, not that you'd be as old as them or anything, but you know . . ."

Lavender leaned her back against the rail, squinted into the sun, and talked not directly to Mary but as if she was speaking to herself. She looked very much like a woman who should be on a luxury cruise liner waiting for an executive husband to come back from a game of deck tennis with the captain.

"I wouldn't apologize or explain too much. Maybe let them think they were part of your lives, even though they weren't. The children should know a bit about them, like their birthdays and their names, and where they grew up themselves. And perhaps you might ask, all of you, about your husband as a little boy, you know, when he was seven or eight, what he read and what toys he played with. They probably have them still. And it could be assumed rather than said that one day, soon, but not a fixed day, the grandparents would come to Ireland."

Lavender seemed apologetic. She felt she had talked too much.

"I wish you wouldn't say you were laying down the law. I'm just overjoyed to get some ideas. That's a very good thought, you know. I don't know their birthdays and the children don't know anything at all about them."

"There'll be plenty of time on the train to London."

"You have children yourself?" Mary was diffident.

"One, a daughter." There seemed to be a full stop.

"That's nice," Mary said. "Or isn't it?"

"Not much at the moment, it isn't."

They had started to walk around the deck. People sat in chairs lathering themselves with Nivea. Duty-free bags were being tucked under the sunbathers, children ran round excited, passengers had all started to talk to each other in the relaxed way of holidaymakers. There might be long drives, or train journeys, or even family ordeals ahead, but on the ship they were suspended. It was time out of time. People spoke, as they often had no time to speak when on land.

"I'm sorry," Mary said to Lavender. "You're so easy, you should have a good time with a daughter."

"I did until she was fourteen. Then she met this lad. Oh, I think a hundred times a day how different life would have been if she hadn't met him.

"She never opened a schoolbook from that day to this. We were before the courts for her every month of the year. If it wasn't truancy it was shoplifting, then it was glue sniffing, then it was a stolen car."

It had certainly not been the life they had hoped for their Emma.

"And did she get over the lad?" Mary sighed, thinking that all this might easily lie ahead for her with Jacinta in a troubled world.

"No, she'll never get over him. She's eighteen now and he's found a new love. So Emma sits and cries. She's sitting down in the restaurant now with her dad, crying. I couldn't take it anymore; she cried all through this holiday in Ireland we took specially to give her a treat. I couldn't see it for one second more. That's why I came up on deck."

"I'm glad you did," Mary said.

"So am I," said Lavender. "But you can see I'm not one to be handing out advice. You see how poor my own situation is. I can't even sit and talk to my own daughter."

"Wasn't it nice of you to bring her to Ireland on a holiday, though?" Mary said admiringly. "A lot of mothers would not have done, with a girl who got into all that sort of trouble. She's lucky."

"She doesn't think so, she thinks she's cursed with middle-aged, old-fashioned parents. She'd like to be left alone with that yobbo."

"Still, she came with you. She's eighteen, grown up, she needn't have come unless she wanted to."

"True." Lavender's face was sad.

"What would be the best that could happen. The very best?"

Lavender was thoughtful. "I used to think if he disappeared off the face of the earth that would be the best. But in their mad white-faced Mohican-hair way with chains dangling and safety pins all over their ears . . . they love each other. So I suppose the best that could happen is for them to love each other without breaking the law and for him to be a bit civil to us. We are part of Emma's life too; for years we held her by the hand and dreamed of what she would do. If he took that into consideration a bit . . ."

"That's why you told me to ask John's parents about the toys, wasn't it?" Mary said.

"Love, it's a different world to yours. You're a lovely warm woman trying to build bridges; he's just a yobbo with a face like the devil trying to break up everything he comes across."

"They must have thought that about me too," Mary said. "I only realize it now. I was so alien and so determined. All the time I was annoyed they couldn't be a bit warmer. But I never thought what it was like

116

to *be* them, having held John's hand for years and listened to his baby talk and watched him starting out to school."

They walked companionably on their tour. They would never meet again, nor write to each other. Mary would never know if the yobbo reformed, or if Emma dried her tears over him. She wouldn't even know what Emma looked like, or her father, who was sitting patiently handing her more and more paper table napkins to wipe the sad, pale, punky face.

And Lavender would never know if the visit went well, and if John's parents took out his old train for John Paul to play with and if Mary became friendly with his mum and helped in the kitchen. She would never hear if the invitation to Ireland, which would be just assumed rather than stated, would in fact be taken up.

Their lives would never cross again.

But while they did cross on a sunny day on a blue sea they talked as all shipboard passengers do in a way that would sound to the seagulls above that these people were friends for life.

And Lavender told Mary that all her sisters had been called after flowers and Mary told Lavender that in her class at school there were eleven girls called Mary and it had been very confusing.

They never knew that their husbands were having a drink at the bar.

Emma's tears had dried, John Paul and Jacinta had found a new friend, and it happened that Lavender's

John and Mary's John were standing having a pint. They talked about golf, they talked about the shambles the World Cup had been, and they talked about prices and Ronald Reagan and trade unions.

And Lavender's John and Mary's John had a second pint and that was it. They were getting near Liverpool now, and so they found their families and their luggage, and one family went north and one went south.

THE
WOMEN IN HATS

*I*t was very exciting watching people come on board, said the purser. After a few journeys you could size them up pretty well. That woman would fight with her husband two days out, he would spend all his time with the bar people, she would find a younger man and a little shipboard romance. That woman over there, she would keep her husband by her side with a rod of iron; she was one of these so-called "invalids" who had nothing wrong with them, except a very serious case of self-importance.

The purser was a beautiful dark-eyed gay Canadian who missed his boyfriend terribly, and rang him from every port and regarded his job as so much torture necessary in order to save enough money for a house on the Great Lakes.

He liked talking to Helen; she was forty and friendly and didn't show any dangerous tendencies of jumping at him some night and assuring him of her powers of being able to make the earth move for him. She played gin rummy with him, told him funny tales about the people at her table, and seemed very interested in his tales of Garry. Helen used to advise him not to call Garry so much. "Telephone calls are very unsatisfactory and expensive," she had said. Paul the nice agreeable purser was beginning to think she was right. He would miss her when she got off at Singapore. He'd have to find a new friend.

Leaning over the side at Piraeus, Paul saw a good-looking man squinting up into the sunshine. A pang of infidelity to Garry swept over Paul, but it was gone as soon as it arrived. Anyway the handsome man didn't look very available. A very beautiful woman with sunglasses in her hair rather than on her face with a golden suntan, and a blue flowing dress exactly the same color as her eyes, seemed to have her hand possessively on his arm.

"What do you make of that pair?" he asked Helen.

"Honeymooners?" wondered Helen.

"No, they don't have that absorbed look," Paul said. "They seem to be talking about something, not just 'Imagine, this is us getting on a ship.' That's the way honeymooners go on."

The tanned girl had a huge blue and white hat tied by a ribbon around her neck. For no reason she annoyed Paul. People should put sunglasses on eyes, and hats on heads. What was she looking at anyway? He followed her gaze.

At the top of the gangway was the fattest woman Paul had ever seen. She wore a huge pink and white hat, on her head, he was relieved to notice. She had a flowing pink and white dress that could easily have been a tent for several people. She carried an enormous beach bag, white but with a name embroidered on it in pink. "Bonnie," it said.

Paul couldn't see her face, but he got the feeling she was young. Immediately Paul felt protective toward her. Even if it wasn't his job, he would look after her. In fact, she might become his friend when Helen left.

"Let's ask the pink elephant lady to have a drink with us?" he said to Helen. "I think she's on her own and she'd appreciate it."

"No," said Helen. "She's not on her own, she's with the non-honeymoon couple—I saw them all get out of the same taxi. But I'm all for a drink with anyone anytime."

Paul looked at Helen with affection. She had talked him out of phoning Garry because of the time difference, the known unreliability of Greek phones, and all the unnecessary angst he would cause himself if there was no reply. Helen must have been through all this love business too, but unlike most women, she didn't seem to want to discuss it or recall it way into the night. Paul called her a purser's joy, someone who didn't complain and who helped other people to enjoy themselves; he said she should really be getting a fee, not paying a fare.

Paul thought Helen must be wrong about big Bonnie. She couldn't be with the golden couple; she wasn't old enough to be the mother, she wasn't young enough to be their child. But when he went to see how they were all settling in, he found the threesome was as Helen had said.

The good-looking boy sat in the middle and on either side of him huge hats bobbed, one blue over the slim tanned girl, one pink over the enormous smiling Bonnie.

"I'm Paul Preston, the purser . . . you are very welcome on board." Bonnie looked up with a big welcoming smile and offered him a huge hand to shake.

"How nice and alliterative," she said. "I'm Bonnie and this is Charlie and this is Charlotte. . . ." She waved delightedly at the golden couple. Paul still couldn't figure out what relation they were to her.

"That's pretty nice and alliterative too," he said about their names.

"I'm always saying that about them," said Bonnie. "It's the most amazing coincidence, my two best friends in the world both called after some no-good Stuart king."

Paul thought it was more of a coincidence that two people called Charlie and Charlotte should have met and married each other than to have turned out to be friends of Bonnie's, but he decided not to follow that line of chat.

They discovered he was from Ottawa originally, would like to live on the Lakes, had been a ship's purser for four years and was aged twenty-nine. He discovered they were from Australia originally, but had lived so long in Europe now they had almost forgotten the Outback. Bonnie was twenty-nine and Charlie and Charlotte were twenty-seven each. Another coincidence. They had been living in Greece for the summer, all three of them, and now they were going to Hong Kong on this ship to see if they could set up a little import-export company, and then they were all going to take a cheap flight back to Australia where they would stay until Christmas. None of them were very enthusiastic about going back home. Bonnie said her parents were dead and she had no ties. Charlie said his father thought people who left Australia were traitors. Charlotte said that her mother wanted her to marry a man who had a big share in a sheep station. They all seemed so easy and relaxed in each other's company that it looked as if they had been friends for years.

Had they been in business long together? he wondered. No, they had only met that spring. All of them had been working in London. Bonnie had advertised for fellow Australians to set up a venture, and that was how they had met.

"And that's how you got together?" said Paul, smiling at the two golden heads of Charlie and Charlotte as they sat together near Bonnie's knees on the deck. They looked like an advertisement for something, so healthy and happy did they seem.

"Yeah, that's how we all met," said Charlie, sounding puzzled.

As the days went on Paul saw no way of making Bonnie into a special friend, since she was never alone. If Charlie and Charlotte, or one of them, weren't with her, she was surrounded by others. She had offered to embroider people's names on their towels or bags, and was doing a roaring trade. Paul was sure that some bylaw said she couldn't charge fees, but he never looked it up.

In Ceylon he bought a beautiful shirt for Garry. Helen had said it was much wiser than spending money on a telephone call, everyone knew how unreliable the Sinhalese telephone service was.

He was admiring the shirt lovingly when a big shadow and a soft footfall came upon him. It was Bonnie.

"Shall I do your name on it?" she asked. "In off white on the pocket, so that you'd have to strain to see it, that would be nice." In fact, that would be very nice. Paul admired her taste.

"Could you put 'Garry' on it?" he asked shyly.

"Is that your boyfriend?" asked Bonnie.

"Well, yes," Paul said. He didn't feel at all at ease with her like he did with nice comfortable, undemanding Helen. In a funny way this enormous woman seemed to consider herself quite socially acceptable. Was there even a hint of a flirtation with him and a sense of regret that there was a Garry in the background?

Paul began to wonder was he losing his reason. He must be imagining it. He must.

They sat in the sunset for a bit, then he told her about the flying fish that sometimes came up on deck, and she told him how much she loved embroidery and sewing and she was going to make herself a huge patchwork cape someday with a hundred colors in it. It would shine out everywhere and nobody could ignore her.

This made Paul strangely uneasy again. With someone like Helen he could have said what came into his mind, which was that he didn't think it a good idea for a gigantic woman to call further attention to herself. He had told Helen several times that she would look nicer if she wore lipstick, and eventually she bought some and wore it just to please him and everyone admired her. He would love to say this to Bonnie, that she should be more restrained, there was no need to go around like a lighthouse. But he didn't dare. Nor did he dare to suggest that she should have white wine and soda instead of the great pint of beer she was drinking as the sun went down.

So Paul didn't become a friend of Bonnie, but he became, to his great amazement, a great observer of her. He noticed the way she settled herself by the swimming pool early with her embroidery, how Charlie and Charlotte would appear and consult her about how the day was to be spent. Bonnie had four sundresses, each one louder and more attention-getting than the one before. Some had sunflowers, some had huge roses, one even had multicolored designs. And there was always a huge hat as well, usually matching the dress. The hat upset Paul most of all. It was like a flag saying "Look at me." It was especially tasteless, he thought, since Charlotte also wore huge hats. Hers looked lovely, they made her seem like a slim Mexican boy, while Bonnie looked like a giant toadstool.

And it wasn't a question of disliking her. She was one of the most easygoing pleasant people he had met. He couldn't work out why he felt uneasy with her. He even discussed it with Helen.

"You've been obsessed with her since they came aboard," said Helen grumpily. "In a way I'm a bit jealous. I don't know why you are doing all this analyzing. It's very simple to understand."

"Well, I wish I understood it," said Paul.

"You want to patronize her, pity her, bring her out of herself, get her to join in things . . . and it isn't necessary. She doesn't need pity, she's already out of herself, she does things without your having to organize it, in fact she's on a nice little number with all that sewing people's names on things. She's taken in a couple of hundred dollars."

Paul thought about this. Well, there was a little truth in what Helen had said . . . just a little. He wasn't upset because Bonnie rejected his friendship . . . it was just that she seemed quite complete without it. That's what was the little pique, the slight wound.

But he was drawn to them all, like someone charmed. He watched them every day, Charlie with his lithe athletic body playing deck games, Charlotte looking like an advertisement for the glamour of cruising, and Bonnie more ridiculous looking, more calm and sure of herself every day. Paul's mother had been fat. Back in Canada she had hardly moved outside her house. But then his mother had been a lady, she had dignity. In a million years she would never have understood this Bonnie who behaved . . . well, like a normal woman.

The words pulled him up short when he felt himself thinking them. Of course, in many ways his mother and Bonnie were normal women, they actually were ordinary people, just fatter than the accepted shape. But Mother had known that it was dignified not to go out and about if you looked different to other people, and when Mother had to go out she wore dark concealing clothes, the most restrained garments she could find. Bonnie with her big mad hats, wide smile, and her red lipstick would have been like a creature from Mars.

He wondered, were Charlie and Charlotte attracted by her in the same mesmerized way as he was? Did they have this mongoose/snake thing with her that he did? One day he decided to discuss it with Charlotte. She was sitting alone for once, feet up on the ship's rail, hat hanging from its ribbon around her neck. She looked very gentle and beautiful.

He wondered, how did Charlie feel able to share her so much? Not that Paul was any authority on women, but he did feel that if you were married to such a dazzling woman as Charlotte you might want her for yourself rather than spend all your time in an odd trio.

"What are you thinking about?" he asked the still girl.

"Oh, I was thinking about how undemanding life is on board a ship. Somebody else decides where you're going, how long you'll stay. I love not having to make any decisions."

"Do you have to make all that many in real life?" he asked.

"Constantly. How to earn money, who to live with, who to trust, where to be, when to leave . . . all the time."

"But that's all over now, I mean you can do it as a team?" asked Paul. He assumed that Charlie must make at least fifty percent of the decisions for the couple.

"Yes, that's the great safety of being with Bonnie," said Charlotte.

"Well, I meant Charlie really," he said.

"Oh, Charlie feels the same, he's often said it to me. He said he felt such a wave of relief when he proposed to her and she said yes. He knew he'd be safe for the rest of his life. . . ."

"When he proposed to Bonnie?" Paul stuttered, confused.

"Well, not proposed, asked her to marry him, whatever people do," said Charlotte. Then suddenly, "What's wrong?"

"I thought you and Charlie were married," he said, "to each other, I mean."

"No, I'm not married to anyone. Charlie and Bonnie were married in spring. You must have known they were married, or together anyway. I mean, they have a cabin and everything. . . ."

Paul was digesting this very slowly indeed.

"I didn't know," he said. Even as he said it he didn't know why he was so shocked. He couldn't sit here and think about it anymore. He got up quickly and made some mumbled excuse—so inadequate that the lovely Charlotte actually sat up in her deck chair to watch him disappearing off down the deck. She shrugged and went back to her book.

Paul found Helen.

"Did you know that he's married to Bonnie, not to Charlotte?" he said.

"Oh yes, I discovered that a couple of days ago. I heard someone call them Mr. and Mrs."

Paul was annoyed that she took it so calmly.

"It's ridiculous. They're so unsuited."

"I think they get on particularly well," said Helen, spiritedly. "I mean, look at the other couples on the ship who are fighting or yawning or sulking. I think Bonnie and Charlie are a tonic."

Paul felt affronted. He was astonished at the violence of his own reactions. He liked them all, he loved none of them. Why should it matter who was hitched to whom? But it did. It really did. He felt very adrift.

Helen looked at him sharply.

"You really have been building up some kind of fantasy about these three, haven't you?" she asked, not unkindly.

"I don't know what you mean," he said defensively.

"You're obsessed by them, and Bonnie in particular. Now, you're the last person on board to realize that it's she who's married to the young blond Adonis. It may have caused a momentary flicker in the rest of us, it's nearly knocked you down."

"I think she's gross," he said suddenly. Helen looked shocked.

"No, of course you don't. She's not nearly as gross as that retiring German missionary who got on at Bombay, and she's not nearly as fat as the Greek woman who has to lift her stomach up in front of her. What can you mean, Paul? She's just a fat girl with a lovely face. You can't ever have looked at her properly if you don't realize that she's absolutely dazzling looking. Just too much fat."

"My mother was very attractive until she let go,"

said Paul in a mulish small-boy voice. "But she never went around in such garish colors calling the full attention of the world to herself."

"Did she go around much at all?" asked Helen with interest.

"No, she had respect for herself. She knew she didn't look well, so she hid herself away. She was very dignified."

"And probably very depressed, too," said Helen very sharply. "How have you the slightest idea whether your mother was dignified or was going nutty as a fruitcake having to stay in the great Canadian indoors just because her pretty little son and her handsome husband might be a teeny bit embarrassed if she ventured out. You don't know anything about anyone."

"You said I was getting upset. You're the one who's shouting now," said Paul, startled by this change in easygoing Helen.

"You make me shout, intolerant insensitive little pansy," said Helen. "Yes, pansy, pouf, queer, I can't remember the other words, but I'm sure they're there. Ten years ago, that's what people would have called you. Ten years ago your particular minority didn't go out very much, it was dignified and depressed and hid itself.

"Stop looking wounded and betrayed. I only say this because you annoy me so much with all your unliberated attitudes. You think it's modern to be able to tell me about Garry . . . think it's just so much rubbish. You can't see that your own mother was a victim to your narrow-mindedness about physical appearance. You want a world of beautiful identical robots. You want a Nazi world, only the fittest and the finest shall be tolerated. . . . You want to grow up, Paul."

Paul was still for a while.

Then he said, "Helen, I don't want to upset you, perhaps you're right, but why do you take it so badly? You're not fat, you can't have an ax to grind for Fat Rights. Tell me what it is that makes you feel so strongly."

"I might have told you once. I might have given in to this seductive shipboard thing of confiding. I thought you were a gentle kind boy with a new open soul. But not now, I'll never tell you. You'll have to guess, and you can spend months guessing, and you'll never know."

Helen laughed at him, not unaffectionately.

"No, little Paul, you'll never know whether I had a fat lover who died from slimming, or whether I was once fat, or whether someone I cared for was hurt by cruel insensitive attitudes such as yours. But that doesn't matter very much. It's just one shipboard story fewer to hear. What does matter is that you realize you are the one out of step, not big Bonnie. She's modern and liberated, she's no prisoner because of her flesh. I don't have an ounce of sympathy for that girl, she's a happy soul, she's got an adoring husband, she's got a good business sense. She's not gross, Paul—you could be. You and Garry could end up in some community where people don't like gays . . . and I'd hate to think where your courage and inner resources might be then."

She gave him an awkward kind of matey hug as she left the room. She didn't want to close every door to him.

With a numbness a bit like the way you feel after having a tooth filled, Paul walked to the upper deck and looked down below. It was sunset, and at sunset every evening, the glorious Charlie sat sipping a drink, flanked by the women in hats, and they were all laughing contentedly in the pinky red light.

EXCITEMENT

*E*veryone said that Rose was immensely practical. She was attractive-looking, of course, and always very well groomed. A marvelous wife for Denis, and wonderful mother for Andrew and Celia. And a gifted teacher. People said that Rose was a shining example. Or if they were feeling less generous, they said that they had never known anyone to fall on her feet like Rose. Married at twenty-five to a successful young man, two children, a boy and a girl, a job to stop her going mad in the house all day, her own car, her own salary every month, no husband grousing about the cost of highlights. Why wouldn't she be a shining example?

It had been Rose who suggested the idea of Sunday brunches. They had all come from the tyranny of family lunches with great roasts and heavy midday meals. So they moved from house to house every Sunday, everyone bringing a bottle of wine and some kind of salad thing. They all dressed up. The children played together. If any couple wanted to bring along a friend, they could.

They congratulated themselves, it kept them young and exciting, they thought. Not dead and lumpen like their parents had been. And it had been Rose's idea in the first place.

Of course, another example of Rose's luck was that her mother lived way down in Cork. She wasn't constantly on the doorstep, criticizing the way the grandchildren were being brought up. Twice a year Rose's mother came up to Dublin; twice a year Rose took the children to Cork. It was yet another example of how well she organized her life.

So they would have been very surprised if they had known how discontented Rose felt as half-term was approaching. She seemed to have been teaching forever. The same things every year, and in the same words. Only the faces in front of her were different, the younger sisters of the children she had already taught.

Then, on the home front, there would be the same arguments with Andrew, six, and Celia, five, about which place to visit when they went to the zoo: Andrew wanted snakes and lions, Celia wanted birds and bunnies. And there would be the same discussions with the au pair. A different name every year, but always the same discussion—the time she came home at night, the long-distance phone calls. And Denis? Well, he was pretty much the same too. There would be the usual jokes about life being a holiday for teachers, about the workers of the world like himself having to toil on. In a million years he would never suggest the two of them went away together. It wouldn't matter what kind of a place. Even a simple guest house. But it wouldn't cross his mind. And if Rose were to suggest it, Denis would say he really shouldn't go away. Business was different from teaching—you had to stay in touch. And then what about Sunday? Surely Rose wouldn't want to miss their Sunday with all the gang? Rose began to wish she had never invented these Sundays. They were a lash for her back.

Always being bright and cheerful, always thinking up a different little dish to make them ooh and aah, blow-drying her hair, putting on makeup, reading the Sunday papers so as not to be out of the conversation, bribing Andrew and Celia to behave. It was always the same.

Rose was quiet as the time came up toward the half-term holiday. Nancy, her friend in the staff room, noticed.

"Where's all the zip and the get-up-and-go?" she asked. Nancy was single and always saying in mock despair that she would never find a man.

"A bit of the magic seems to be going from it all," Rose said more truthfully and seriously than she had intended to.

"Maybe he has the seven-year itch," Nancy said. "A lot of men get it just because they think it's expected of them. We poor spinsters keep reading about such things just so that we'll be ready for marriage, if it ever comes. It'll pass, though, it usually does."

Rose looked at her in disbelief. Really, Nancy was as thick as the wall. It wasn't Denis who had a seven-year itch. It was Rose. She was thirty-two years of age and, for the foreseeable future, her life was going to be exactly the same as it was now. A lifetime of smiling and covering her emotions had made Rose very circumspect. She was, above all, practical. There was no point in having a silly row with her friend and colleague Nancy.

"Maybe you're right, let's hope that's all it is," she said with her mind a million miles away from the mild expression on her face. Because Rose now realized the truth. She was restless and unsettled. She was looking for something, a little spark, a little dalliance. Possibly even a little affair. She felt a shiver of excitement and disbelief. She wasn't that kind of person. She had always thought wives who strayed were extraordinarily foolish. They deserved all they got, which was usually a very hard time.

Rose found that, in the days that followed, everything had become even more samey than it used to be. Denis said, "Sorry, what was that?" to almost every single sentence she spoke to him, sometimes not waiting until she had finished. Every day Maria Pilar said, "I mess the buzz, the buzz was late." It was useless to tell the stupid girl that either she was late or the bus was early. Rose gave up trying. Andrew said every day that he hated cornflakes and Celia, to copy him, said the same thing. Rose's mother phoned from Cork regularly to say how good the life was down there, how dignified, gracious, and stylish compared to the brashness, vulgarity, and violence of Dublin. Rose listened and murmured, as she felt she had been doing for years. A meaningless murmur.

And then it was Sunday again. She prepared a rice salad with black olives and pine nuts for the gathering at Ted and Susie's. She knew before they even rang at the door what Susie would say. Susie, a colorless woman who would have looked very well if she had dyed her eyelashes and worn bright colors, in fact did say, exactly as Rose had known: "How clever you are, Rose. You always think of marvelous things. I don't know how you do it."

Rose had the urge to scream at her that occasionally she opened a bloody cookbook, but stifled it. It would not be practical to shout at a friend, a hostess. She smiled and said it was nothing. She went into the room—there they all were, each playing the role that could have been written for them.

Bill was talking about the match, Gerry about the cost of airfares, her Denis was nodding sagely about Business Expansion Schemes, Nick was telling them about a horse he knew. And the women had roles, too. Annie talked about the litter in the streets, Nessa about the rudeness of the people in the supermarket . . . Susie, as she always did, apologizing and hoping everything was all right.

Rose's mind was a million miles away when Ted, standing beside her and spooning some of the rice salad onto his plate, said into her ear: "Very exotic."

"Oh, it's quite simple, really," she began mechanically.

"I didn't mean the rice, I meant you," he said, looking straight at her.

Ted. Ted with the new car every year and the fairly vague job description, married to mousy Susie, who had the money.

"Me?" Rose said, looking at him with interest.

"Well, your perfume, it's very exotic indeed. I always fancy that if we were all in the dark I'd find you immediately."

"Well, it's hard to prove seeing that it's broad daylight." She laughed at him, her eyes dancing like his.

"But it won't be daylight on Tuesday," he said. "Not in the nighttime, that is."

"Now, *what* made you make a deduction like that?" She was still playful but didn't sound puzzled or outraged. It was as if she were giving him permission and encouragement to go on.

"I'm going to Cork on business . . . overnight . . . and I thought that perhaps we could test out this theory of the perfume, you know. See whether I knew what part of the room you were in. What do you think?"

It was the moment to ask did he mean to include anyone else. It didn't need to be asked. "And have you thought out how this could be managed?" she asked. She spoke in her ordinary voice, as if they were talking about any of the same things they talked about in each other's houses for the last seven years.

"I gave it a load of thought," said Ted, "like it's your half-term and you could be staying with your mother, as it were." He was leaning on a shelf and looking at her. Interested. That's what he looked. It was a lovely, almost forgotten feeling to have someone looking at her like that. Rose felt a tightening of her throat, and a small lurch in her stomach.

"You've thought of everything," she said.

"I don't see any obstacles, do you?" Ted might have been talking about garden furniture.

"Only the messy one of upsetting people," she said.

"Ah, but you and I wouldn't do anything like that. It's not as if we're falling in love or leaving anyone or breaking up any happy homes. It's just a bit of . . . well, how would I describe it . . . ?"

"A bit of excitement?" Rose suggested.

"Precisely," he said.

145

She thought it was very sophisticated of them indeed not to make any plans and think up any cover stories. If it was going to happen, which she thought deep down it would, then these would all come later. They rejoined the group.

Rose let her glance fall over the others, Nessa and Susie and Annie, Grace. Did none of them ever ache for a little excitement in their lives? And if they did, whom would they have found it with? Hardly her own Denis. He had barely time and energy for that kind of activity in his own house without thinking of arranging it with someone else's wife. The Sunday ended, as every Sunday did, with a visit to the pub. They had their traditions in this too. No big rounds, meaning that people stayed all night. Each family bought their own drink. It was very civilized, like everything they did. And very, very dull, Rose realized.

As they left the pub for the car, Andrew said he hated fizzy orange, and Celia, who had drunk very little other than fizzy orange in her life, said she hated it too.

Denis opened the door of the car for Rose. "Don't we have marvelous friends?" he said unexpectedly. "We're very, very lucky."

She felt a hard knot of guilt form in her chest. But she swallowed it and agreed.

"But we work at it, of course," Denis said. "Having friends means a commitment of time and effort."

Rose looked out the window. If working to achieve a Sunday exactly like this every single week was the result of time and commitment, then she was absolutely within her rights to want a day off, a night out.

The knot of guilt had quite disappeared.

Ted rang casually and told her there was a great place to leave her car in for an overhaul, only a few miles beyond Newlands Cross. Rose took down the details and thanked him. If the call had been bugged by every private detective and secret service in the world, it would have seemed totally innocent. Rose went into town and bought herself a black lace nightdress, a bottle of full-strength perfume with matching talcum powder, and body lotion. If she was going to have a bit of excitement with Susie's handsome husband, he was going to remember it for a long time.

"I want to go to the zoo tomorrow," Celia said at supper.

"That sounds nice," said Denis, not looking up, "Mummy's on half-term."

Rose looked at her son, hoping he would speak on cue. He did. "I hate the zoo," Andrew said.

"I hate the zoo too," said Celia.

"That's settled, then. Maria Pilar will take you out for a lovely walk and an ice cream."

"I get tired when I go on a lovely walk," said Andrew.

"So you can go on the buzz. Maria Pilar loves the buzz."

"Eet is not the buzz, eet's the bussss," said Maria Pilar, hissing across the table.

"So it is, I keep forgetting." Rose got up briskly

147

from the supper table. "Now, I've got lots to do, I'm off to see Grannie tomorrow."

"I want to see Grannie," Celia said.

"I hate Grannie," Andrew said. Before Celia remembered that she hated Grannie also, Rose said no, this was a flying visit.

"Are you taking the plane?" Andrew asked with interest. His hatred of his grandmother might be tempered by a new experience like going in an airplane.

"Sorry, what was that, you're going to see the old bat?" Denis asked.

"Has Grannie got a bat?" Andrew was very interested now.

"I want to see the bat," Celia said.

Rose glared at her husband. Now she would have to pretend that Grannie did have a bat. "It's out a lot," she said. "Especially at night."

"It's too much down and back in one day," Denis said.

"I know, I'll stay the night." Rose was surprised how easy it came when it had to, the lie, the cover-up. She always thought that women who weren't used to this would bluster or redden and give themselves away.

"You're doing your purgatory on earth, that's all I can say." Denis left the supper table and went into what they called his Denis's Den. He would be there until midnight. There were a lot of figures to be sorted out—coming up to sales conference time, he would tell her if she protested. Or Annual Report time or the AGM or the Visiting Firemen. There was always something.

Rose slept a guilt-free sleep. No woman was meant to sign on for such a dull life. That had been part of no bargain. Somewhere in the air there was a little clause allowing for a few Excitements along the way.

Ted was waiting exactly where he had said at ten o'clock. He was relaxed and easy. They transferred Rose's little overnight bag into his trunk.

"This is great fun," he said.

"Isn't it just?" said Rose.

On the journey, they flirted with each other mildly. Rose said he drove the car in such a masterful way. Ted said she curled up like a kitten in a very seductive way. They played Chris de Burgh tapes. Ted had to do a few calls, but he had booked a table for lunch somewhere he thought Rose would like. Perhaps she'd like to settle into the hotel first and meet him at the restaurant. They didn't mention Denis or Susie. They told each other none of the cute little things said by Andrew and Celia or by Ted and Susie's children. This was an Excitement, time out and away from all that.

Rose examined the bedroom with approval. . . . She hung up her good dress, hid all the perfumed unguents in her case. She didn't want it to look as if everything had come out of a bottle. She looked at her own face in the mirror. She was exactly the same as she had been last Sunday morning, only two days ago before Ted had come up with the offer of the Excitement. The same, but a little more carefully groomed. She had waxed her legs. Always a dead giveaway about affairs, people said, but Denis wouldn't have noticed. She strolled happily along to the restaurant, where she was greeted by a cry that froze her blood. "Rose, Rose, over here." It was her mother.

Sitting with Nora Ryan, the most horrible person in the South of Ireland or maybe in the whole of Ireland. A woman with beady eyes and a tongue that shot in and out like a snake's tongue. Delivering harsh, critical words every time. They were sitting at a table for three, and they pulled out the third chair for her. Rose felt a pounding in her head. It was if they had expected her.

"How did you know I was . . . um . . . coming to see you . . . ?" she stammered.

"Well, I rang. I rang and that not very bright girl said you were in zee Cork."

"Europeans," said Nora Ryan, casting her eyes up to heaven.

"We're all Europeans," snapped Rose before she could stop herself.

"How observant of you, Rose dear," said Nora Ryan with three flashes of her thin, serpentine tongue.

"And what did you say?" Rose spoke to her mother.

"I said that's great, and that Nora and I were having lunch here, but that stupid girl couldn't understand a word I said.

"Spaniards!" said Nora, her eyes nearly reaching the brim of her hideous hat.

"So what did you do then?" Rose felt a sense of blind panic that she had never known before.

Now the unthinkable had happened. Her mother must have told her husband there had never been any question of a visit. Was there a hope in hell Rose could pretend it had been meant as a surprise?

"I had a very odd conversation with my grandson, who seemed to think the house was infested with bats and that you were coming down to deal with them." Rose put her head in her hands. "So then obviously I rang Denis at the office to find out what was happening."

"And what did he say?"

"Questions, questions, really, Rose, you're like one of these interrogators on television," said Nora Ryan.

Rose flashed her a look of pure loathing. "Mother, what did Denis say?"

"He said he was well, he said he was busy coming up to the sales conference. . . ."

"Before I have to take you by the throat and beat it out of you, Mother, what did he say about my coming to Cork? What did he say?"

"Really, Rose," Nora Ryan began.

"Shut up, Mrs. Ryan," said Rose.

They stared at her. Rose tried to recover the lost ground. She spoke very slowly, as if talking to someone of a very low IQ. "Can-I-ask-you-Mother-to-tell-me-what-did-Denis say?"

Rose's mother was fingering her throat, the one that Rose had threatened to shake her by. She seemed almost afraid to speak. "I don't see *why* you're talking like this, Rose, I really don't. I told Denis that if you called before you went out to the house this is where we'd be having lunch. To save you . . . to *save* you the journey out to the house . . . that's what I was doing and inviting you to lunch in a nice smart place like this. . . ." Rose's mother had taken out a handkerchief and dabbed the corner of her eye. "I most certainly didn't expect dogs' abuse and interrogation about it." She was hurt and she didn't mind them knowing it.

Mrs. Ryan was now in the totally unaccustomed role of being a consoler. "Now now, now now now," she said, patting the shaking shoulder awkwardly and flashing glances of hate at Rose.

"Did he know I was coming to stay with you?" Rose's voice was dangerously calm; the words came out with long spaces between them.

"Of course he knew," her mother sniffled.

"How did he know?"

"I told him."

"How did *you* know, Mother?"

Rose's mother and Nora Ryan looked at each other in alarm. Perhaps Rose was going mad . . . seriously mad.

"Because Maria Pilar had told me, my grandchildren had told me. . . ."

The breath seemed to come out of Rose more easily now. "Yes. Well, that's fine, that's all cleared up," she said.

And at that moment Ted came into the room, carrying a single red rose wrapped in cellophane. The blood drained from her head yet again.

He saw her and came over. "What a surprise. What a huge surprise," he shouted like a very bad actor in an amateur play.

The two older women looked at each other; again their alarm increased.

"Good God . . . it's Ted," cried Rose. "Of *all* the people in the world!" She looked around the room as if she expected to see a few other equally unexpected people, like Napoleon.

"I'll tell you the most extraordinary thing," Ted shouted, unaware that the entire dining room was now looking at them and could not avoid listening to them.

"This is my mother," screamed Rose. "My mother that I was coming down to Cork to visit."

"How do you do?" Rose's mother began, but she might as well have been talking to the wall.

"The *most* extraordinary thing," Ted repeated. "I was back at the hotel before . . . um . . . before coming alone here, and who did I meet but Susie's brother and his wife. Susie is my wife," he said to the sixty or so people who were now part of his listenership. "They are in Cork and staying in the same hotel." He paused to let the words sink in with all the diners. "The very same hotel." He didn't get the reaction he wanted, whatever it might have been, so he said it in a different form. "The *selfsame* hotel, I think you might say," he said triumphantly.

Rose began to babble. "That's lovely for you, Ted, you can all be together. I'd love to stay in a hotel myself sometime, but I'm staying with my *mother*."

Mrs. Ryan looked at her with narrowed eyes. "I'm sure your mother wouldn't mind at all if you were to stay in a hotel," she said pleasantly.

"No, no, no, I can't. And anyway, Mother has a lot of bats in the house," she floundered wildly to Ted, "so that's where I'll be staying."

Ted might not even have heard her.

"So the odd thing was that when they thought they saw me, they asked at Reception was that me and Reception, of course, goddamn interfering nosy parkers that they are, said that Mr. *and* Mrs. Ted O'Connor were there."

Rose said, "What did you do?"

"I told them that suddenly at the last moment Susie couldn't come and then Reception said did I want to move to a single room because it would be cheaper, and I said yes, but that I'd rush up and pack my things and so I did and they're in the back of the car, if you know what I mean."

Rose looked at him. His face was scarlet; he looked like a madman talking to other very mad people.

"If you get my drift," he roared.

Rose felt a sudden maturity sweep over her. She knew now that she had enough excitement to last her a long time. On the grounds that she was helping Ted

154

to park his car, she left with him, retrieved her suitcase. They were both too shocked to speak.

She returned to the restaurant, where the diners looked up with interest, hoping for Round Two.

Ted had given the red rose to Mrs. Ryan. "I bought it for you," he had said without explanation. Nora Ryan saw nothing odd in this. In her youth it had happened a lot, she said.

Rose spoke courteously to her mother, planned the night in the house that she had forgotten was bat free and worked out what train to get back to Dublin and how to retrieve her car from beyond Newlands Cross. To begin what she hoped would be a fairly even-tempered and unexciting period of her life.

HOLIDAY WEATHER

*R*obert said that after dinner they would curl up with the map of the South of France and plan the journey. Frankie was looking forward to it. This was always a great part of the holiday, when he would sit on the sofa with his arm around her, the fire crackling in the grate, glass of wine at hand, and together they would point out magical names to each other. It had been like this last year, when his conference had been in Spain and they had hunted for little Spanish idylls for their rambles afterward. And the year before, when it had been in Italy, and their fingers had traced the names by the lakes.

Of course, Frankie knew that the evening would not organize itself. She would have to escape down to the shops at lunchtime to buy something she knew he would like, and this was getting more difficult since he had begun to worry about his waistline. Gone were the evenings of fillet steak, mushrooms, and garlic bread. Perhaps she might get some monkfish—very expensive, but it did seem special—and a small selection of vegetables. She could even top and tail them at work; there would be so little time when she got back to her flat. She would have to rush around it tidying, of course, getting rid of all the work things that littered the place. Well, Robert hadn't been around for over a week, so she had been doing her Open University course every evening.

Frankie thought happily about the evening ahead. She would wear her green dress, the one that he had once said matched her eyes. A long while ago. But of course he still loved her, and people didn't have to go on about eye color forever. It would have been unnatural, and possibly a bit repetitive.

The only good thing about working for a man like Dale was that it took up such a small amount of time and so little brain. All that the awful Dale wanted was someone to sit in his front office and look pleasant, ask them to wait a moment while they could thumb through some of the fairly horrible cuttings about Dale's success in the world of public relations, and then ask them to go straight on in. Frankie was far too intelligent for this job, and that knowledge alone gave her great satisfaction. But by being with Dale and his outfit, she had an excuse to see Robert almost every day. And as far as Frankie was concerned, she would work in a coal mine or as a steeplejack if it meant being close to Robert.

Robert needed excuses to meet Frankie. Robert was married to his boss's daughter—a marriage of convenience that he had entered into at a time before he knew what true love, real love, was like.

Robert and his wife had two children, who were eight and seven. They were at the age when they could not be upset by things that had nothing to do with them; it wasn't their fault that Robert had found true love too late. Robert was the rising star in the organization; he must work harder than ever now that he intended to leave home and set up two establishments. He must make himself totally indispensable to his boss, his father-in-law, so that there would be no question of letting him go once the divorce was brought up. Frankie didn't ask when that was going to be but thought that it would be unreasonable to expect it before the children went to boarding school. Three years, perhaps?

She would wait. Naturally.

But in the meanwhile there were wonderful things like the great summer honeymoon. They always called it that: Our Italian, Our Spanish, and now Our Riviera Honeymoon.

Frankie made her shopping list and took out the map of France. Whenever Dale passed by she looked as if she were making notes or looking up a reference. Dale would not stop to question her.

Frankie looked fine for the job, with her long dark curly hair and her bright green eyes. And even more important, she was the friend of Robert the whiz kid in Benson's. Dale would have employed any kind of person in that front desk if it kept him well in with Benson's. He regarded it as a bonus that Frankie was both bright and beautiful.

The only thing that bored Frankie was that she had to put in the actual hours in her horseshoe-shaped desk. If only she could have slipped away for the afternoon. She could have gone to the hairdresser and even had a manicure as a luxury; her hands would be greatly in view tonight as they traced the route south through the Côte d'Azur down from Cannes past St. Raphael to Saint-Tropez. Or should they go the other way from Cannes, over past Antibes to Nice and Monte Carlo? It was heady stuff even saying the names. Perhaps Frankie would even buy a little guidebook at lunchtime so that she would appear knowledgeable tonight.

It was all a rush, as she knew it would be. But the dinner had gone well. Robert was relaxed; he had loosened his tie and kicked off his shoes. Frankie had been able to wash her hair, and she had bought green earrings at lunchtime.

"They're lovely," he said. "The color of your eyes."

She felt that the fuss and the bustle had all been worthwhile. She even felt glad that she had spent that money on a dishwasher. It had been very extravagant, but Robert adored it. His wife was playing Earth Mother, according to his reports, refusing modern gadgets, but for them it was all right—there was the help and the au pair. In Frankie's flat, however, he loved to see technology. Cuts out all the fuss, he had said. They arranged the china and glass and cutlery carefully and listened to it humming away in the kitchen as Frankie got out the map.

"Darling," he said. "Wrong map, I'm afraid."

"It says Provence on top, but it's all Cannes and Nice and everywhere down on the coast," Frankie said, surprised. Normally Robert knew where everywhere was; that was why she had studied it so much in advance all afternoon.

"We're not going, my love," he said.

Her heart lurched with the kind of jump that almost reached her throat.

"I don't understand."

"Neither do I, but it's true. Listen, don't think I'm pleased. . . . Stop looking at me like that, hey?"

"Why can't I come? We've always been able to swing it before. I tell Dale I'm taking my vacation, you tell Mr. Benson you need someone from Dale's to run over the implications of the conference with you. Why can't I come this time? Why?" Frankie knew she was sounding like a seven-year-old, but her disappointment was so huge she couldn't hide it.

She had bought her clothes, her terribly expensive shoes, the knockout beach gear. The operation was foolproof—why was he pulling out now? Was it possible that he had found someone new? If he had cheated on his wife once, then obviously he could do it again. But don't go down that road. And don't *cry*. Frankie forced her face to stop puckering.

Robert sounded weary and resigned.

"It's not you, sweetheart, it's me. It's a nonstarter."

"But you always go to the conference. You *are* Benson's." She was aghast. And yet there was a seed of hope. Suppose he had been discovered, and maybe even demoted. Did that not mean that the day they could be together might be nearer than they had thought?

"This year being Benson's means going somewhere else and shoring up someone else's cock-up," he said. "A whole project is going down the Swanee, and apparently I'm the only one who can sweet-talk us back where we were. What a bloody crowd of fools he employs. I'd have got rid of three quarters of them. I will—I tell you I will one day."

This was an old refrain. Frankie didn't want to hear it all over again—Robert's plans for the day when he ran the place himself. This was an old set of lines they had said to each other; she wanted to know what was new.

What was new was Ireland. A new plant, a lot of bother, nobody had been there to straighten it out, to tell the people on the ground what was happening, what was expected of them, what they could expect.

"They're bound to be suspicious of us, think we're in it for what we can get out of it."

Frankie said nothing; for once she didn't murmur her usual words of encouragement. In fact, she knew that Benson's was in it for what they could get out of it, that's what business was about.

"So you see what's happened. In the very week of the conference in Cannes, I have to be over in the middle of the boglands talking to the mutinous forces over there and promising them wealth beyond their wildest dreams."

"Can't you go now? Before the conference?"

"Don't you think I asked that? But old man Benson is adamant. It has to be that bloody time, something to do with some European thing or other that's being held there. They're much more interested in Europe over there, for some reason that escapes me. God, I could kill them for not setting it up right at the start, allowing all these discontents to grow up. If we don't go in and fly the flag or show our face or whatever the expression is . . . then the whole thing could collapse like a house of cards." He looked so handsome when he was annoyed. She could understand why so many people were impressed with him.

"Will we have any honeymoon together this year, you and I?" she asked in a small voice, looking down at the ground lest he see all the pain in her green eyes.

"You could come to Ireland," he said doubtfully. "I can't be tied up with them all the time. We'd have some time together."

"To do what?" She had no maps of Ireland, she had no magical names like Juan les Pins, like Saint-Tropez.

"I don't know, darling, I don't know, give me space. I only heard about this today, this afternoon. We'll do something. It could be a rest for you, getting away from it all, and then I'd escape when I could."

A more courageous woman would have told him to forget it. A tougher woman would have told him in no uncertain terms what he could do with this half-hearted offer.

Frankie was neither brave nor tough. Which was why she found herself in the small hotel on the west coast of Ireland. A hotel called the Greener Grass standing on a low cliff over a long, empty beach. When you looked across that sea the next stop was America, they told you. Frankie could believe it—it looked endless. And on the first days it looked gray and lonely. The seagulls calling to each other and other seabirds coming in to perch on rocks. She saw a school of porpoises go by one day, and she became familiar with the habits of a cormorant and a kittiwake and a tern and a gannet.

"I could do another Open University course in the

habits of seabirds," she said ruefully to the proprietor as he set her lobster before her at a table, which, for the third time had been set for one.

"There are worse ways to spend your time, you know." His voice was soft, but it was distant. He was Shane, he said, a returned Irish American. He had called his place the Greener Grass because of the grass always seeming greener when it was far away. He had saved up for seven years to buy his own small hotel.

He was different from the other local people, who wanted to know all about Frankie and Robert, and what was their business in the place, did they have any children, where had they been for holidays before. Did they love the Irish way of life? Shane asked none of these questions. He had the air of someone contented with his own way of life. She saw him choosing his own vegetables from the fields where he had tilled the land to grow them. She watched him sometimes writing the menus in slow, careful, calligraphic script.

Robert set out in the early mornings and was rarely back to the Greener Grass before dark.

"Not much of a honeymoon, is it, darling?" he said more than once. Frankie saw his face, white and tired.

"The honeymoon bit is at night, remember?" she said, laughing.

But at night the weary Robert slept suddenly and soundly as soon as he got into bed. Some nights Frankie sat at the bay window, where there was a lovely three-part window seat, and looked out at the night sky over the water. Sometimes she saw Shane and his dog Tracey walking.

So he couldn't sleep either, Frankie thought, even though he had saved seven years to build his dream and had it now in his hands.

She saw Shane bend to pick shells by the moonlight. He looked peaceful, she thought, and somehow at ease. Even though he didn't really belong here, not like locals—he had been away too long, and he had a slight New York tinge to his voice.

Next morning at breakfast, she asked him about the shells.

"You sat at the window and looked out over the moonlit sea," Shane said. Robert seemed annoyed somehow. "You didn't tell me you couldn't sleep." She felt she had been disloyal.

Later Shane came and gave her some cowrie shells. "You could do another Open University course on these and still know nothing about them," he said with a smile.

Robert liked to think that it was somehow a rest for her, that sharing some fraction of his life was reward enough for the broken promise, the conference that never was . . . the ribbon of the French coast not visited.

"I bet this is doing you no end of good," he said each morning as they ate brown soda bread and fish just in from the sea.

For the first few days she had smiled bravely, and taken a book disconsolately to walk along the hilly cliff or down to the rock pool, and try to stop thinking that her life was as gray as the skies all around her.

But then one morning the sun came out, and everything was different. Even Robert seemed loath to go.

"It's very beautiful, this place, you know," he said as he stood beside his hired car about to head off for the day with the mutinous men he was finding it harder to placate than he had thought possible.

Frankie looked down at the beach she had walked so often in the dull days. Today it sparkled, as if there were little particles of precious metal hidden behind the rocks instead of soft sand. She thought she could see the cowrie shells that Shane had been collecting. The sea was twenty different colors of green and blue, with little white flecks.

"I might have a swim," she said.

"Yes, well, be sensible. It's the Atlantic Ocean, don't forget."

"Next stop, America." Frankie laughed.

Robert looked at her, puzzled.

"I hope I won't be too late," he said, but doubtfully. "This lot seem to need conversation and explanation way into the night, as well as all day."

He drove away along the road, and as Frankie looked after him up at the purple mountains and over beyond the small green fields with their stone walls to a dark, velvety forest, she began to feel as if a film had just turned from black-and-white into Technicolor.

She ran lightly upstairs to fetch the red bathing suit that had cost her so much in the days she thought it would be seen on the Côte d'Azur. As she came down, carrying the pricy beach bag and her red and white fluffy towel, Shane's dog Tracey came up and looked at her hopefully.

"I'd be very grateful if you would," Shane said. "He needs a walk, and with today's weather I'll have the world and its wife for lunch, so I can't take him."

"I don't know a lot about dogs," Frankie began.

"Well, Tracey is half sheepdog and half setter, we think. A lovely nature, and he'll bark if you start to drown or if anyone comes and bothers you."

"Who'd come and bother me?" Frankie laughed, looking at the empty beach.

"I haven't seen you in that swimsuit, but it might attract a bit of local attention." He laughed too; the good weather made him seem less remote.

"Would he run away or get into a fight or anything?" It had never been part of her life, walking with a big, bounding dog.

"Not a chance. And as a reward, I'll come and find you and take you a little late lunch and take Tracey off your hands."

"Oh no."

"Oh yes. It's the minimum fee for dog minding. There's a nice flat rock in the next bay. It makes a good table."

She had never spent a day on a beach like it. Tracey ran for sticks with never-ending energy. She really thought she could see his foolish face smile at her as she threw them again and again.

Tracey barked at the waves, but swam in and paddled near her as if to look after her when she swam. She collected shells and laid them out on the flat table rock.

Soon, far sooner than she had expected, Shane arrived with a picnic basket.

"You abandoned your lunchers. How can you expect to earn a living!" she said sternly.

"You're not wearing a watch. It's after three o'clock—they've all been and gone. You must be starved."

Imagine. She had been playing with this idiotic dog for hours on a shell-covered beach, no cloud had come across the sky, and no thought of Robert and their situation had come across her mind.

Companionably they shared the picnic, local prawns, homemade bread, cheese made by some nuns in a convent across the valley, red shiny apples from the small orchard behind the Greener Grass.

"It's like heaven." She sighed as they drained the bottle of wine to the dregs.

"Thank God we don't get weather like this all the time," said Shane.

"Why do you say that? Because you'd have to work too hard?" Frankie had been about to say the very opposite; she had been on the point of wishing that every day could be so sunny.

"Because we would be parched and dry, it would not be a green island, and we'd be so used to it we wouldn't be calling out our thanksgiving to the very heavens as we are today," he said.

"Yes, I know, and that's a point, but what about your business? If it was much sunnier, there would be many more people here. This beach would be full."

"And could you and I and Tracey have had such a picnic if the beach were full?" he asked.

"We had meant to go to the South of France," she said suddenly.

"Yes, so your husband told me, when he called to book." Shane had his distant face on again. "He seemed very disappointed and told me in several different ways that this was not his first choice."

Frankie was going to explain that Robert was not her husband, but she let it go. Instead she apologized for him.

"He's normally very charming and would never have given you that impression. He has work problems to see to here. We had thought we could have made a holiday out of a conference in Cannes."

"But why did he take you here, and leave you all alone?"

"I'm glad he did," Frankie said positively. "Now, do you think it's an old wives' tale about not swimming after lunch, or should we risk it?"

"Just as long as we don't go out too far, any of us," he said, and they raced to the edge where the foam was breaking and drawing out the sand with it as it gathered for another wave.

"Have you ever been to the South of France?" he asked.

"No." Her voice sounded small.

"Neither have I, so let's pretend this is a hundred thousand times better," Shane cried, and threw himself into the waves.

"You caught the sun," Robert said when he got back earlier than usual. He had phoned to ask if dinner could be kept for him, and had been surprised and not altogether pleased to hear Shane say that his wife had had a late lunch.

"Did you tell him we were married?" Robert asked as they sat at a window table and watched the sun set, leaving red and golden paths and crisscross lines across the bay.

"No, darling, I didn't, but in this country they are likely to assume it if we check in to the same room and you have booked us as 'Mr. and Mrs.' "

Robert looked at her sharply but decided not to make it something to argue about.

"Is it better? You know, are you sorting it out up at the plant?" Frankie asked.

"Yes. I think they believe our heart is in the right place," Robert said.

"And it is?" Frankie's face was innocent, bland.

"What are you trying to say?"

"Well, I mean that a lot of them came back from jobs overseas because they really believed that it was going to be a proper plant, not something that would pack up and fold its tent when things got a bit hairy."

"Oh, come on, Frankie, what do you think Benson's is, part of Mother Teresa? Of course we have to be practical. If things get hairy, as you put it, we can't stay on here forever, bleeding hearts keeping returned emigrants in beer money."

"That's all right, as long as they know it."

"That's all right whether they know it or not," Robert flashed.

"You remind me more and more of Dale," Frankie said. "The same cynical way of looking at everything."

"You are beginning to remind me more and more of my wife. The same way of picking a row and nagging over everything."

Frankie had read somewhere that you know when something is over, you know that this is the moment, but you won't accept it. You try to say it was because one person had too many tiring days negotiating, and the other person had too much unexpected sun.

Robert probably knew, too, because when he was called to the phone he went with eagerness and came back to say that some of the men needed him for a further conference.

They parted pleasantly, almost with relief.

Frankie went walking on the beach in the last rays of the sun. She felt Tracey rushing up to her before she knew Shane was on the beach as well.

"I had a friend in New York, a great friend, she was

going to come here and run the Greener Grass with me. You know, a joint enterprise. Then she said she'd join me later. Then she said she needed thinking time. Then she said she'd write."

They walked in silence; there seemed no need to say anything. Frankie thought about all those years, and those two honeymoons where she had felt she needed to entertain Robert all the time, talk to him, be bright, show no hurt, no loneliness.

"He's not my husband," she said after a long time.

"Oh, I know," said Shane.

"How?"

"Labels on suitcases, his instructions about not ever calling him to the phone if the office rang but always taking a name and a time he should call at. If you were married, he would have asked you to take the messages."

After another long time Frankie asked, "Is it all right? You know, running the place as a single venture, not a joint one as you had thought?"

"Yes, it's all right. It mightn't always be single. You never know your luck."

The sea was calm now. They skimmed flat stones and made them hop.

"He'll be going back soon, I imagine," Shane said. "The lads tell me it's all settled."

"Yes, well, they wouldn't want to rely on that too much."

"They're smarter than they sound," Shane said

with a laugh. "All us fellows who worked over the water learned a bit about business."

"We had planned to stay on a bit when it was settled, but I don't think so now."

"No, he'll want to be off. He might even catch the tail end of the Cannes thing."

"A place where the sun shines all the time and there's no sense of surprise?" Frankie smiled at him.

"The very spot," Shane said.

"And what's the weather forecast like here?" she wondered.

"Optimistic but unknown," said Shane.

"I'll stay," said Frankie. "I'll certainly stay on awhile until I know how it turns out."

They walked back to the Greener Grass in a companionable silence, because they knew there was no need to say anything, or plan anything, or spell anything out, or indeed say anything at all.

VICTOR AND ST.
VALENTINE

*V*ictor was brought up in a home where they made a huge fuss of St. Valentine's Day. His sisters spent weeks wondering if anyone would send them a card; his mother cooked a very special meal for her husband that evening and served it by candlelight. His father bought something romantic like a heart-shaped charm for her bracelet, a little pendant, a glass vase for a single rose.

No wonder he thought it was a speical day.

In the real world, he discovered, things were different. At school, for example, fellows didn't send girls cards unless they were jokey ones, often with hurtful remarks on them.

Nobody made any mention of St. Valentine's Day ceremonies in their homes, so Victor stayed quiet about his own household. No point in *inviting* mockery. It was quite enough that he was already the subject of a lot of ridicule because of gentleness, good manners, and a lack of interest in beating up his classmates in the playground.

Then, later, when he went to train as an electrician, they did make a bit of a fuss and celebration at Technical College for a St. Valentine's Day dance but mainly the chat was about which girls would be likely and which would not.

Victor never wanted to talk about people being likely; he thought it was too personal a thing to be speculated over in the bars. So the others more or less gave up on him in this area.

His first boss was not a man with much time for St. Valentine. A load of commercial claptrap, he said.

Around that time Victor sent a valentine card to a nice girl called Harriet who had gone to the pictures with him several times. Harriet telephoned him at once.

"Listen, Victor, I'm sorry, there has been some awful misunderstanding. I wasn't being serious or committed or wanting to marry you or anything." Victor was alarmed.

"No, heavens no, neither was I," he said, panicking at the very thought.

"Then why did you send me this card with all the roses and violets and sign your name?" she asked.

"Because it's St. Valentine's Day," he said.

"But you signed your own name. Naturally I thought you wanted commitment." Harriet was outraged at the misunderstanding.

"I'm very sorry," Victor said humbly. "I'll never do it again."

But of course he did do it again, when he met Muriel, and did fancy her greatly.

Muriel said he should have had the courage to come straight out and say it if he loved her and rather than relying on a card and somebody else's verses and sentiments. She couldn't see a future for them. She was sorry.

Victor decided he was not good with women. He wasn't without dates, a social life, and indeed the odd little romance, but none of them led to anything.

He was, however, a very good electrician. He had a pleasant manner and a lot of skill, and soon he didn't have to have a boss at all—he had his own business. A mobile phone, a business card, and a lot of word-of-mouth recommendation, and Victor had more customers than he could deal with.

Sometimes they asked him about his private life. "Never met the right woman for me," he would say.

"And here I am a hopeless romantic. But the girls don't take me up on it at all."

He was thirty-eight, tousled hair, a warm smile.

People didn't really believe him. They thought that he might have a very colorful private life but just wasn't telling.

People liked Victor and told him things. And he liked listening to them, because in his own way he was a little lonely.

He would have liked a companion to go out with on weekends. Someone to go on vacation with.

Victor had saved money for a holiday, but it wasn't quite the same going alone. So he enjoyed talking to his clients. Like the couple who were going to adopt a baby, and were so excited when it arrived that they invited Victor to the welcome party.

"Are you a relation?" somebody asked him.

"No, but I rewired the nursery," he said, and again nobody believed him.

And there was the man who dared not tell his wife that he had been made redundant; Victor had many a cup of tea with him on a day when he was merely meant to be putting in new sockets.

And mainly there was old Mrs. Todd.

She was very fond of Victor. She told him all about her family, her son Frank who was so protective of her that he had set up this door-entry system where she could see on a little screen who was there before letting them in. Mrs. Todd hadn't wanted it all, but her son Frank had insisted; the world was full of bad, dangerous people, he said.

Frank didn't come much to visit his elderly mother, which Victor thought was a pity, but Frank laid down the law a lot from a distance. Mrs. Todd said that Frank had given instructions she was not to invite any new people that she met to coffee. This was hard, but she was sure Frank must be right.

Victor thought Frank sounded like a bully but was too tactful to say so. Frank's daughter, Amy, had gone off to Australia as soon as she was old enough to leave.

Mrs. Todd said that Amy wrote regularly; she lived in Sydney, she worked in a flower shop there, and she was very happy. She wished that her gran would come out and see her.

"Why don't you go?" Victor encouraged her.

He was in Mrs. Todd's appartment yet again over an allegedly loose connection. He knew and she knew that there was nothing wrong electrically speaking, but that she was very, very lonely. He would arrange to call on her at a time that suited him to when he was in the area, and she paid him a token fee to keep the thing on some kind of professional basis.

"Oh, I couldn't go for lots of reasons," she said. "I'm not really able to travel on my own, and anyway it would be a bit awkward. You know Amy doesn't get on with her father, so even if I were strong enough to travel there alone, it would cause a family upset, and we don't want that."

Vincent sent her a Valentine's Day card, but after his earlier frights in such matters, he didn't sign it.

It was on her mantelpiece when he next called to check the mythical mystery of the immersion heater.

"Thank you so much for the valentine, Victor," she said.

"What makes you think I sent it?"

"Apart from my late husband, you are the only really romantic person I know," she said.

The months went on. Her son Frank appeared less and less and gave yet more and more directions.

The letters from Amy were more and more yearning. "Please come out here, Gran, I want to show you my Australia. You are not old, because you have a young heart. I'm saving to send you the fare."

Around Christmas, when it was cold and wet in London, Victor made a decision.

"Mrs. Todd, why don't you and I go there early next year together? I'll deliver you to your granddaughter, then I'll go off and see a bit of the Outback. I might hire a car and drive to Broken Hill. I'd enjoy that. Then I'd come back and take you back home."

Her eyes filled with tears.

"You are such a kind man, even to *think* of it. Believe me, that's enough to make me very happy."

"No, Mrs. Todd, you must believe me, this is for me as much as you. I've always wanted to go to Australia. I've had the money saved and waiting, I just couldn't find the excuse."

"But Frank?"

"Frank will have to accept it."

"No, Victor. That's easy for you to say, you're a young man. I'm an old woman. Frank is all I have. He wouldn't dream of letting me go out all that way with . . . with . . ."

"With the electrician," Victor finished for her.

"Well, yes, in a word."

"Then I'll have to be a friend of Amy's, that's what we'll say."

They smiled at each other. The adventure had begun.

It didn't take long to become a friend of Amy's, much less time than anyone would have thought possible, and all because of E-mail.

Every morning he got a message from her. It was nighttime in Sydney, and Victor sent one back, before she went to sleep. Bit by bit they put together the subterfuge, they invented a way in which they had met and become friends. They rejoiced at each other's inventiveness.

She said nothing hostile about her father, but made it clear that they were people who, while minimal courtesies would be maintained, would never have a meeting of the minds.

Frank was told, as he had to be, about the upcoming trip. He had a dozen objections, all them rehearsed, and answered by the three conspirators. But he was up against unequal odds.

And then they were on the plane. Mrs. Todd and

Victor. They laughed when the steward thought they were mother and son.

"No, we are partners in an enterprise," Mrs. Todd explained.

They drank Australian wine to get into the mind-set of the New World. They slept and woke.

And slept. They got out for coffee in the Middle East and for Tiger Beer in Singapore. Neither of them thought it the slightest bit odd to travel together to a continent on the other side of the earth.

They watched movies, they read magazines, and they talked about their past. Mrs. Todd told Victor about Mr. Todd, who had been a wonderful, kind man who brought flowers home every Friday night and had told her she looked like a flower herself.

Victor told Mrs. Todd about the various ladies in his life and how he had been a little too romantic for them. Perhaps his luck would change. No he didn't, he didn't really think it would in Australia. They were very modern there, forward looking, they would think he was a silly old Pom.

Mrs. Todd said there were romantic people every-where in the world, and he must not make generaliza-tions.

Then it was dawn, and they saw the Opera House and the Bridge and all the things they had dreamed of, and they landed.

Crowds waited in the sunshine.

Victor wheeled Mrs. Todd out in her chair.

A girl with a wonderful smile was waving at them.

She had on pink shorts and sunglasses. Long black curly hair, dimples in her cheeks.

He knew immediately it was Amy.

"We're here," he shouted.

"It's about time," she called back.

Mrs. Todd and her granddaughter embraced each other. They hugged and cried, and looked at each other with amazement. Around them the same scene was being acted over and over again. Australians welcoming the relatives from Britain.

Victor the electrician stood a little apart. Then they remembered him.

"This is Amy," said Mrs. Todd with huge pride.

"Welcome to Australia," said Amy. She had a warm smile.

Suddenly he wished he hadn't made such firm arrangements about leaving Sydney to drive to the Outback. Sure it would be exciting, and that was one of the reasons he had come all this way. But Sydney looked as if it had a lot to offer as well. And he had only given himself three days to see it.

Amy showed them the city in style. She drove them over the famous Harbour Bridge and got them on a ferry to sail under it. She rightly regarded nothing as being too tiring or adventurous for her elderly grandmother.

She brought them to small restaurants where she knew the Greeks and Italians who ran the place. She liked that, it was all so international, she said.

"London's getting like that, too," Victor said.

"Oh, London." Amy shrugged.

"They're not all like your father," Victor said before he could stop himself.

But she only smiled.

"Just as well," she said.

They had pretended to be old friends as a ruse to fool her father. Already they felt they *were* old friends.

He longed to give her a valentine's card before he drove off across the bush, down the ribbon road that would take him past scrubland and ostriches. Amy had told him to be very careful of the kangaroos at sunset, they could jump out in front of the car. But Victor reminded himself of the many times his greetings had been misunderstood.

Perhaps there was a chocolate koala bear with hearts on it. But then, there was no point in sending a jokey thing; he couldn't understand a whole industry based on that.

He wanted to say thank you for lighting up our lives. Why should it have to be dressed up as a joke?

He came to say good-bye, and Amy handed him a single red rose. There was a card on it: "I'll miss you, Victor Valentine."

When he could speak, he said, "I was thinking I needn't stay away all that long."

Amy said, "And I was thinking maybe we might come with you."

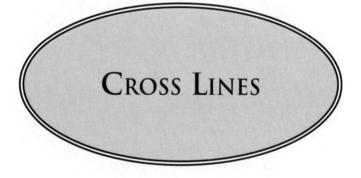

CROSS LINES

*M*artin tapped his fingers in irritation on the phone. He was unsure of himself in his new and unfamiliar world of the arts where he was heading. There were already too many stresses involved in this whole business without having to part from Angie in such an unsatisfactory way. Beautiful Angie, why hadn't she got up and pulled on a track suit? Why hadn't she said she'd drive him to the airport, they'd have coffee and a croissant together; it would have been so good. It would have calmed him down, to have sat with Angie, looking into her big dark eyes watching the passersby envy him with this girl with the great mane of streaked hair and the big slow smile. He would have felt a million times more confident about the venture ahead. Instead of edgy and jumpy.

In the next booth he saw one of those kind of career women he disliked on sight. Short practical hairdo, mannish suit, enormous briefcase, immaculate makeup, gold watch pinned to a severe lapel. She was making a heavy statement about being equal and coping in a man's world. She was having a heated discussion with somebody on her telephone. Probably entirely unnecessary, shouting at someone for the sake of it. He would give Angie another three minutes and dial again. She had never been known to talk this long to anyone. And at nine-thirty A.M.

Kay wished the man in the next phone box would stop staring at her; she had enough to cope with with one of Henry's tantrums. She had explained to Henry over and over how important it was for her to be at the trade fair a day in advance; that way she could supervise the setting up of the stand, make sure they had the right position, the one they had booked near the entrance, see that the lighting was adequate, decorate the booth, get to know the neighbors on her right and left so that she could rely on them and call on their support once the doors opened and the day's business began.

Henry had said he understood, but that was yesterday; today he was in one of his moods.

Kay would be gone for five days; she *hated* leaving him like this, it was so uncalled for, he had nothing to fear from her trip to another town. She would be far too weary and exhausted to consider going out partying at the end of a long day; all she would want was a warm little telephone conversation every night, reassuring her that he loved her, that he was managing fine but not so fine as he managed when she was around and how he greatly looked forward to Friday. She had called him at the office to try to dispel his mood before it got a grip of him.

It had been a mistake. Henry's black disapproval came across the phone line loud and clear.

She had made her choice. She had decided for an extra day on this junket, and against going with him to his staff party. It was quite simple; she could take the consequences.

"What consequences?" Kay shouted, turning her back on the arty pseudo-bohemian in the next phone box.

He was handsome, she supposed, in that vain peacock way that a lot of actors or showbiz people adopt, mannered and self-aware, stroking his cravat. The kind of man she most disliked. But it was increasingly hard to talk to Henry, the kind of man she most admired. He was showing none of those qualities that had marked him out when she met him first.

He pointed out that if Kay, his constant companion, was not going to bother to turn up at an important corporate gathering, then he would regard himself as a single and unattached person with no commitments.

"That's blackmail of the worst kind." Kay was appalled at herself for reacting like a teenager.

"The solution is in your hands," Henry said coldly. "Come back from the airport now and we will forget the whole incident." She hung up immediately, not trusting herself to speak to him.

Martin told himself that Angie's deep sleep was always important to her. She was a model; her face had to be unlined, untired at all times. She must have taken the telephone off the hook. His brow cleared when he remembered this, only to darken again when he remembered that as he kissed her good-bye he had said he would call from the airport and she had said that would be super. Why, then, had she cut off his way of getting through to her?

Lost in their thoughts, neither Martin nor Kay realized that they had in fact been seated beside each other on the plane. . . . They looked at each other without pleasure. Martin took out the long, complicated report on arts funding that he was going to have to explain to various theatrical and artistic organizations, all of which were going to brand him as a cultural philistine. Kay read a report on last year's trade fair, and noted all the opportunities missed, contacts

194

lost, and areas of dissatisfaction. Their elbows touched lightly.

But they were unaware of each other. From time to time they lifted their eyes from the small print in their folders and Martin thought of all the times *he* had driven Angie to her modeling assignments and Kay remembered all the corporate functions in *her* firm that Henry had refused to attend without even the flimsiest excuse.

Above the clouds it was a lovely day, bright and clear. Kay felt her shoulders relaxing, and some of the tension leaving her. They were far above the complications and bustle of everything they had left behind: buildings, traffic, rush, corporate functions. She breathed deeply. She wished they could stay up here forever.

At that moment Martin sighed too, and with the first sign of a pleasant expression that he had shown, he said that it was a pity they couldn't stay up here forever.

"I was just thinking that. At exactly this moment," Kay said, startled.

They talked easily, he of the problems ahead trying to convince earnest idealistic artists that he was not the voice of authority spelling out doom for their projects. He had been trying to dress like arty people, as he knew that otherwise he would be dismissed as a Man in a Suit, which was apparently marginally better than being a child molester.

She told him of the poor results the company had achieved at last year's promotion, and how this was her first year in charge. There were many in the organization who hoped she would fail, and she feared they would be proved right. She knew that people thought she had got the post through some kind of feminine charm; she was dressing as severely as she could to show them that she wasn't flighty.

They were sympathetic and understanding. Martin told her what Henry never had, that perhaps she was overcompensating, making herself look too stern and forbidding, killing off the good vibes she might otherwise have given.

Kay told Martin something that Angie had never thought of—that possibly the cravat might be over the top. There was the possibility that the disaffected artistic folk might think he was playing a role.

They fell into companionable silence in the clear, empty blue sky. And Martin thought that Angie probably didn't care about him at all, she cared only about her face, the magazine covers she appeared on, and what bookings her agent might have for her next week. He would call her when they landed, a cheerful call, no accusations about taking the phone off the hook, she would wish him well, and he would take the whole thing much more lightly from now on.

Kay wondered if Henry would seriously take up with someone else, as he had threatened. And would she mind very much if he did. She decided she would ring Henry's secretary and say how sorry she was to miss this evening's function, she would wish it well and say that sadly work had taken precedence. She would ask that Henry not be disturbed but insist that her message of goodwill was passed to those in the right places. This was a professional businesslike approach, not a very loving one. But Kay didn't feel very loving anymore.

Then just at the same moment she and Martin left their private thoughts and turned to each other to talk again. Angie wasn't mentioned, nor was Henry, but strategy was, and optimism was exchanged.

Kay encouraged Martin to be straight with the groups, to tell them the worst news about funding first and try to work back into a position they felt was marginally more cheerful. Martin advised Kay to let her colleagues in on her hopes for their joint success, let them think they were creating it too. By the time they left the plane they were friends in everything but name. Martin considered asking her name but thought it might sound patronizing. Kay wondered about giving him her card but feared it would look stereotype female executive.

There was a bank of telephones facing them in Arrivals. They both headed toward them.

Kay paused with her hand on the receiver. In the next box she saw Martin's fingers, not drumming this time but hesitating. Through the transparent walls they smiled at each other.

He looks less affected, she thought, the velvet jacket's fine really.

She is quite elegant in spite of all that power dressing, he realized.

Neither of them made the phone call.

But it was too soon for any sudden decisions. There was work to be done. If they met each other somewhere again, well and good.

They wished each other luck and got into separate taxis.

As they settled back into their separate seats they each gave their taxi driver the name of the same hotel.

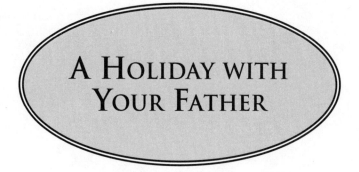

A HOLIDAY WITH
YOUR FATHER

*R*ose looked at the woman with the two cardboard cups of coffee. She had one of those good-natured faces that you always associate with good works. Rose had seen smiles like that selling jam at fetes or bending over beds in hospitals or holding out collection boxes hopefully.

And indeed the woman and the coffee headed for an old man wrapped up well in a thick overcoat even though the weather was warm, and the crowded coffee bar in Victoria Station was even warmer.

"I think we should drink it fairly quickly, Dad," said the woman in a half-laughing way. "I read somewhere that if you leave it for any length at all, the cardboard melts into the coffee and that's why it tastes so terrible."

He drank it up obediently and he said it wasn't at all bad. He had a nice smile. Suddenly and for no reason he reminded Rose of her own father. The good-natured woman gave the old man a paper and his magnifying glass and told him not to worry about the time, she'd keep an eye on the clock and have them on the platform miles ahead of the departure time. Secure and happy, he read the paper and the good-natured woman read her own. Rose thought they looked very nice and contented and left, cheered to see a good scene in a café instead of all those depressing gloom scenes you can see like middle-aged couples staring into space and having nothing to say to each other.

She looked at the labels on their suitcases. They were heading for Amsterdam. The name of the hotel had been neatly typed. The suitcases had little wheels under them. Rose felt this woman was one of the world's good and wise organizers. Nothing was left to chance; it would be a very well planned little holiday.

The woman had a plain wedding ring on. She might be a widow. Her husband might have left her for someone outrageous and bad-natured. Her husband and four children might all be at home and this woman was just taking her father to Amsterdam because he had seemed in poor spirits. Rose made up a lot of explanations and finally decided that the woman's husband had been killed in an appalling accident that she had borne very bravely and she now worked for a local charity, and that she and her father went on a holiday to a different European capital every year.

Had the snack bar been more comfortable, she might have talked to them. They were not the kind of people to brush away a pleasant conversational opening. But it would have meant moving all her luggage nearer to them, which seemed a lot of fuss. Leave them alone. Let them read their papers, let the woman glance at the clock occasionally, and eventually let them leave. Quietly, without rushing, without fuss. Everything neatly stowed in the two bags on wheels. Slowly, sedately . . . they moved toward a train for the south coast. Rose was sorry to see them go. Four German students took their place. Young, strong, and blond, spreading coins German and English out on the table and working out how much they could buy between them. They didn't seem so real.

There was something *reassuring*, she thought, about being able to go on a holiday with your father. It was like saying thank you, it was like stating that it had all been worthwhile . . . all that business of his getting married years ago and begetting you and saving for your future and having hopes for you. It seemed a nice way of rounding things off to be able to take your father to see foreign cities . . . because things had changed so much from his day. Nowadays young people could manage these things as a matter of course; in your father's day it was still an adventure and a risk to go abroad.

She wondered what her father would say if she set up a trip for him. She wondered only briefly, because really she knew. He'd say:

"No, Rose my dear, you're very thoughtful, but you can't teach an old dog new tricks."

And she would say that it wasn't a question of that. He wasn't an old dog. He was only barely sixty, and they weren't new tricks since he used to go to Paris every year when he was a young man, and he and Mummy had spent their honeymoon there.

Then he would say that he had such a lot of work to catch up on, so it would be impossible to get away, and if she pointed out that he didn't really have to catch up on anything, that he couldn't have to catch up on anything, because he stayed so late at the bank each evening catching up anyway . . . Well, then he would say that he had seen Europe at its best . . . when it was glorious, and perhaps he shouldn't go back now.

But he'd love to go back, he would love it. Rose knew that. He still had all the scrapbooks and pictures of Paris just before the war. She had grown up with those brown books, and sepia pictures, and memos and advertisements, and maps carefully plotted out

. . . lines of dots and arrows to show which way they
had walked to Montmartre and which way they had
walked back. He couldn't speak French well, her father, but he knew a few phrases, and he liked the
whole style of things French, and used to say they
were a very civilized race.

The good-natured woman and her father were
probably pulling out of the station by now. Perhaps
they were pointing out things to each other as the
train gathered speed. A wave of jealousy came over
Rose. Why was this woman—an ordinary woman perhaps ten years older than Rose, maybe not even that—
why was she able to talk to her father and tell him
things and go places with him and type out labels and
order meals and take pictures? Why could she do all
that and Rose's father wouldn't move from his deck
chair in the sun lounge when his three-week holiday
period came up? And in his one week in the winter, he
caught up on his reading.

Why had a nice good warm man like her father got
nothing to do, and nowhere to go after all he had
done for Rose and for everyone? Tears of rage on his
behalf pricked Rose's eyes.

Rose remembered the first time she had been to
Paris, and how Daddy had been so interested, and
fascinated, and dragging out the names of hotels in
case she was stuck, and giving her hints on how to get
to them. She had been so impatient at twenty, so intolerant, so embarrassed that he thought that things
were all like they had been in his day. She had barely

listened, she was anxious for his trip down the scrapbooks and up the maps to be over. She had been furious to have had to carry all his carefully transcribed notes. She had never looked at them while there. But that was twenty, and perhaps everyone knows how restless everyone else is at twenty and hopefully forgives them a bit. Now at thirty she had been to Paris several times, and because she was much less restless she had found time to visit some of her father's old haunts . . . dull, merging into their own backgrounds . . . those that still existed . . . she was generous enough these days to have photographed them, and he spent happy hours examining the new prints and comparing them with the old with clucks of amazement and shakings of the head that the old bakery had gone, or the tree-lined street was now an underpass with six lanes of traffic.

And when Mum was alive she too had looked at the cuttings and exclaimed a bit and shown interest that was not a real interest. It was only the interest that came from wanting to make Daddy happy.

And after Mum died people had often brought up the subject to Daddy of his going away. Not too soon after the funeral, of course, but months later when one of his old friends from other branches of the bank might call . . .

"You might think of taking a trip abroad again sometime," they would say. "Remember all those places you saw in France, no harm to have a look at them again. Nice little trip." And Daddy would always smile a bit wistfully. He was so goddamn gentle and nonpushing, thought Rose, with another prickle of tears. He didn't push at the bank, which was why he wasn't a manager. He hadn't pushed at the neighbors when they built all around and almost over his nice garden . . . his pride and joy, which was why he was overlooked by dozens of bed-sitters now. He hadn't pushed Rose when Rose said she was going to marry Gus. If only Daddy had been more pushing then . . . it might have worked. Suppose Daddy had been strong and firm and said that Gus was what they called a bounder in his time and possibly a playboy in present times . . . just suppose Daddy had said that. Might she have listened at all or would it have strengthened her resolve to marry the Bad Egg? Maybe those words from Daddy's lips might have brought her up short for a moment . . . enough to think. Enough to spare her the two years of sadness in marriage and the two more years organizing the divorce.

But Daddy had said nothing. He had said that whatever she thought must be right. He had wished her well, and given them a wedding present for which he must have had to cash in an insurance policy. Gus had been barely appreciative. Gus had been bored with Daddy. Daddy had been unfailingly polite and gentle with Gus. With Gus long gone, Rose had gone back to live in Daddy's house. It was peaceful despite the blocks of bed-sitters. It was undemanding. Daddy kept his little study where he caught up on things, and he always washed saucepans after himself if he had made his own supper. They didn't often eat together . . . Rose had irregular hours as a traveler and Daddy was so used to reading at his supper . . . and he ate so early in the evening. If she stayed out at night there were no explanations and no questions. If she told him some of her adventures there was always his pleased interest.

Rose was going to Paris this morning. She had been asked to collect some samples of catalogues. It was a job that might take a week if she were to do it properly or a day if she took a taxi and the first fifty catalogues that caught her eye. She had told Daddy about it this morning. He was interested, and he took out his books to see again what direction the new airport was in . . . and what areas Rose's bus would pass as she came in to the city center. He spent a happy half an hour on this, and Rose had looked with both affection and interest. It was ridiculous that he didn't go again. Why didn't he?

Suddenly she thought she knew. She realized it was all because he had nobody to go with. He was in fact a timid man. He was a man who said sorry when other people stepped on him, which is what the nicer half of the world does . . . but it's also sometimes an indication that people might be wary and uneasy about setting up a lonely journey, a strange pilgrimage of return. Rose thought of the good-natured woman and the man who must be ten or fifteen years older than Daddy; tonight they would be eating a meal in a

Dutch restaurant. Tonight Daddy would be having his scrambled egg and deadheading a few roses. while his daughter, Rose, would be yawning at a French restaurant trying not to look as if she were returning the smiles of an aging lecher. *Why* wasn't Daddy going with her? It was her own stupid fault. All those years, seven of them since Mummy had died, seven years, perhaps thirty trips abroad for her, not a mention of inviting Daddy. The woman with the good-natured countenance didn't live in ivory towers of selfishness like that.

Almost knocking over the table, she stumbled out and got a taxi home. He was actually in a cardigan in the garden stratching his head and sucking on his pipe and looking like a stage image of someone's gentle, amiable father. He was alarmed to see her. He had to be reassured. But why had she changed her mind? Why did it not matter whether she went today or tomorrow? He was worried. Rose didn't do sudden things. Rose did measured things, like he did. Was she positive she was telling him the truth and that she hadn't felt sick or faint or worried?

They were not a father and daughter who hugged and kissed. Pats were more the style of their touching. Rose would pat him on the shoulder and say: "I'm off now, Daddy" or he would welcome her home clasping her hand and patting the other arm enthusiastically. His concern as he stood worried amid his garden things was almost too much to bear.

"Come in and we'll have a cup of tea, Daddy," she

said, wanting a few moments bent over kettle, sink, tea caddy to right her eyes.

He was a shuffle behind her, anxiety and care in every step. Not wishing to be too inquisitive, not wanting, but plans changed meant bad news. He hated it.

"You're not *doing* anything really, Daddy, on your holidays, are you?" she said eventually once she could fuss over tea things no longer. He was even more alarmed.

"Rose, my dear, do you have to go to hospital or anything? Rose, my dear, is something wrong? I'd much prefer if you told me." Gentle eyes, his lower lip fastened in by his teeth in worry. Oh, what a strange father. Who else had never had a row with a father? Was there any other father in the world so willing to praise the good, rejoice in the cheerful, and to forget the bad and the painful?

"Nothing, Daddy, nothing. But I was thinking it's silly my going to Paris on my own. Staying in a hotel and reading a book and you staying here reading a book or the paper. I was thinking wouldn't it be nice if I left it until tomorrow and we *both* went. The same way . . . the way I go by train to Gatwick . . . or we could get the train to the coast and go by ferry."

He looked at her, cup halfway to his mouth. He held it there. "But why, Rose dear? Why do you suggest this?" His face had rarely seemed more troubled. It was as if she had asked him to leave the planet.

"Daddy, you often talk about Paris, you tell *me*

about it, I tell *you* about it. Why don't we go together and tell each other about it when we come back." She looked at him . . . he was so bewildered she wanted to shout at him, she wanted to finish her sentences through a loudspeaker.

Why did he look so unwilling to join? He was being asked to play. Now, don't let him hang back slow to accept like a shy schoolboy who can't believe he has been picked for the team.

"Daddy, it would be nice. We could go out and have a meal and we could go up and walk to Montmartre by the same routes as you took in the Good Old Days. We could do the things you did when you were a wild teenager. . . ."

He looked at her, frightened, trapped. He was so desperately kind, he saw the need in her. He didn't know how he was going to fight her off. She knew that if she were to get him to come, she must stress that she really wanted it for her, more than for him.

"Daddy, I'm often very lonely when I go to Paris. Often at night particularly I remember that you used to tell me how all of you . . ."

She stopped. He looked like a hunted animal.

"Wouldn't you like to come?" she said in a much calmer voice.

"My dear Rose. *Sometime*. I'd love to go to Paris, my dear, there's nothing in the world I'd like to do more than to come to Paris . . . but I can't go just like that. I can't drop everything and rush off to Paris, my dear. You know that."

"Why not, Daddy?" she begged. She knew she was doing something dangerous, she was spelling out her own flightiness, her own action of whim of doubling back from the station . . . she was defining herself as less than levelheaded.

She was challenging him, too. She was asking him to say why he couldn't come to a few days of shared foreign things. If he had no explanation, then he was telling her that he was just someone who said he wanted something but didn't reach for it. She could be changing the nature of his little dreams. How would he ever take out his pathetically detailed maps and scrapbooks to pore once more with her over routes and happenings if he had thrown away a chance to see them in three dimensions?

"You have nothing planned, Daddy. It's ideal. We can pack for you. I'll ask them next door to keep an eye on the house. We'll stop the milk and the newspaper, and, Daddy, that's it. Tomorrow evening in Paris, tomorrow afternoon we'll be taking that route in together, the one we talked about for me this morning. . . ."

"But, Rose . . . all the things here . . . my dear, I can't just drop everything . . . you do see that."

Twice now he had talked about all the things here that he had to drop. There was *nothing* to drop. What he would drop was pottering about scratching his head about leaf curl. Oh, Daddy, don't you see that's all you'll drop. But if you don't see and I tell you . . .

it means I'm telling you that your life is meaningless and futile and pottering. I will not tell *you*, who walked around the house cradling me when I was a crying baby, you who paid for elocution lessons so that I could speak well, you, Daddy, who paid for that wedding lunch that Gus thought was shabby, you, Daddy, who smiled and raised your champagne glass to me and said: "Your mother would have loved this day. A daughter's wedding is a milestone." I won't tell you that your life is nothing.

The good-natured woman and her father were probably at Folkestone or Dover or Newhaven when Rose said to her father that of course he was right, and it had just been a mad idea, but naturally they would plan it for later. Yes, they really must, and when she came back this time they would talk about it seriously . . . and possibly next summer.

"Or even when I retire," said Rose's father, the color coming back into his cheeks. "When I retire I'll have lots of time to think about these things and plan them."

"That's a good idea, Daddy," said Rose. "I think that's a very good idea. We should think of it for when you retire."

He began to smile. Reprieve. Rescue. Hope.

"We won't make any definite plans, but we'll always have it there, as something we must talk about doing. Yes, much more sensible," she said.

"Do you really mean that, Rose? I certainly think

it's a good idea," he said, anxiously raking her face for approval.

"Oh, honestly, Daddy, I think it makes *much* more sense," she said, wondering why so many loving things had to be lies.